RUNAWAY COWGIRL BRIDE

TRIPLE J RANCH BOOK 3

JENNA HENDRICKS

BOOKS BY JENNA HENDRICKS

Triple J Ranch –

Book 0 - Finding Love in Montana (Join my newsletter to get this book for free)

Book 1 - Second Chance Ranch

Book 2 – Cowboy Ranch

Book 3 – Runaway Cowgirl Bride

Book 4 – Faith of a Cowboy (coming soon)

<u>Big Sky Christmas</u> –

Book 1 – Her Montana Christmas Cowboy

Book 2 – Her Christmas Rodeo Cowboy

See these titles and more: https://JennaHendricks.com

OTHER BOOKS BY J.L. HENDRICKS (MY 1ST PEN NAME)

Worlds Away Series

Book 0: Worlds Revealed (join my Newsletter to get this exclusive freebie)

Book 1: Worlds Away

Book 2: Worlds Collide

Book 2.5: Worlds Explode

Book 3: Worlds Entwined

A Shifter Christmas Romance Series

Book 0: Santa Meets Mrs. Claus

Book 1: Miss Claus and the Secret Santa

Book 2: Miss Claus under the Mistletoe

Book 3: Miss Claus and the Christmas Wedding

Book 4: Miss Claus and Her Polar Opposite

The FBI Dragon Chronicles

Book 1: A Ritual of Fire

Book 2: A Ritual of Death

Book 3: A Ritual of Conquest

See these titles and more at https://www.jlhendricksauthor.com/

NEWSLETTER SIGN-UP

By signing up for my newsletter, you will get a free copy of the prequel to the Triple J Ranch series, Finding Love in Montana. As well as another free book from my other pen name, J.L. Hendricks.

If you want to make sure you hear about the latest and greatest, sign up for my newsletter at: Subscribe to Jenna Hendricks' newsletter. I will only send out a few e-mails a month. I'll do cover reveals, sneak peeks of new books, and giveaways or promos in the newsletter, some of which will only be available to newsletter subscribers.

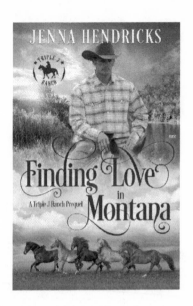

JENNA HENDRICKS

Finding Love
in
Montana

A Triple J Ranch Prequel

TABLE OF CONTENTS

RUNAWAY COWGIRL BRIDE

A woman unsure why she's in white. A man who offers the comfort she needs. Will a traumatic beginning bless them with a happily-ever-after?

The only thing Claire Brown feels is confusion. After waking up on the side of the road with no memory, she's stunned that she's wearing a wedding dress. Praying for deliverance, she's overjoyed when a handsome cowboy pulls over and offers his assistance.

Matthew Manning is a perfect gentleman. So when he stumbles upon a bride suffering from amnesia, he doesn't hesitate to offer shelter at his family's ranch until she can recall her identity. But with no ring on her finger and no one searching for her, he can't help but want to be the man she deserves.

As an undeniable attraction forms between Claire and the rugged rancher, she begins to believe God placed this kind soul in her life for a reason. And the more Matthew's interest in her grows, the more he fears a groom suddenly arriving to claim the woman he's come to cherish.

Will a forgotten marriage stop true hearts from beating together?

Runaway Cowgirl Bride is the third book in the uplifting Triple J Ranch cowboy Christian romance series. If you like sweet notions of good will, men of faith, and lessons from the Lord, then you'll adore Jenna Hendrick's darling tale.

CHAPTER 1

"Hank, Mimi, thank you so much for your hospitality. I've enjoyed seein' your ranch." Matthew Manning smiled at his hosts and loaded his last bag into the truck.

"It's been our pleasure, Matthew. It's so nice to have a friend visit." Mimi Walton smiled at her old friend and wished he wasn't leaving already. "When you get home, tell my sister she needs to come and visit soon. I miss her."

"Wasn't she just here, visitin' a few weeks back?" Matthew arched a brown brow. He knew that Mimi missed her family, especially her sister, Harper Bensen, but he also knew that Harper spent most of her vacations here with her sister since Mimi married Hank.

A pretty pink hue covered Mimi's cheeks, and she put a protective hand across her stomach.

A lightbulb went off in Matthew's head. "Ah, I see." He nodded and patted Hank on the shoulder. "Congratulations, my friend. Somethin' tells me you won't be comin' to Beacon Creek for a visit any time soon." His loud chuckle filled the air around them.

Hank joined in, and Mimi smiled and sighed. "He's being

a caveman. Insisting that I don't ride or go anywhere farther than town."

Hank slid his arm around his wife. "This is my first baby. I plan on being very overprotective. Count on it." He leaned over and kissed the top of his wife's head.

A pang filled Matthew's heart. Until recently, he'd been happy being single. But with everyone getting hitched lately, he had started to think about finding his own wife. The only trouble: none of the cowgirls in town interested him. And he certainly wasn't going to use a dating app. He'd heard nothing but bad things about them. Most of the women were either looking for a good time or a rich husband. He wasn't going to fill either bucket.

"I hope you're ready for lots of visitors. I expect y'all be seein' lots of folks from home who'll want to come visitin' once the wee one's born." He knew it was too soon to know the sex of the baby. And no matter what, he only wanted a healthy baby for the couple.

He'd known Mimi most of her life, and her younger sister, Harper, was best friends with his sister, Elizabeth. Even though Lizzie was now married, he expected his sister would want to be here for the birth, or shortly thereafter.

"We've got plenty of guest rooms in this huge house. Everyone is welcome." The extra glow on Mimi's face made more sense now.

Matthew had thought she looked better than he'd ever seen her before, and now he knew why. He wanted to rub at the phantom pain in his chest. He knew there wasn't anything wrong with him except for the hollow feeling inside. But he knew that part of him was missing his other half. That was how Elizabeth had described it to him once.

She'd said that she knew Logan was her other half because when they weren't together, part of her heart was missing. He'd never understood what she meant until recently. Matthew hadn't loved and lost anyone, but he did think he was ready to settle down. His mother told him many times that it was high time to marry and begin a family. Two of his siblings had beaten him to the punch.

Well, Luke wasn't married yet. The only reason he and Callie hadn't tied the knot yet was because she wanted to finish her first year as a sheriff's deputy before she took any time off. Mark, one of his other brothers, had begun harassing Matthew and even went so far as to make a bet with Luke that Matthew would get married first. He'd laughed when he heard their silly bet. But deep down, he wanted to be the first man in the group of brothers to marry. He was the oldest, after all.

His thirty-second birthday was coming up in a month. Not that he was worried, but he didn't want to be an old man when his youngest child graduated. Matthew had come from a large family and he couldn't imagine not having a herd of children of his own.

Growing up, his ranch had been the place for his friends to come and hang out. While he wasn't the only one to have a lot of siblings, his family loved to entertain and all the town's kids were welcome at their place. Weekend barbecues were the norm while he was growing up. When the weather was good, they could easily have up to twenty or thirty kids and their parents over for the day.

His family ranch, The Triple J, was known to have the best-quality and tastiest beef in the state of Montana, so they always provided the meat. But their neighbors would bring plenty of side dishes when they came over, and most of the spring and summer weekends were spent at his ranch. He wanted to continue the tradition and hoped for at least four children of his own. If he wanted to be a decent age to enjoy rambunctious children like he and his brothers had been, then he'd have to get started soon.

The only problem: he wanted to marry for love. Men didn't talk about their emotions with one another, but he knew his father married for love. His best friend, Logan, had married his sister Elizabeth for love. And he knew beyond a shadow of a doubt that Luke would be marrying Callie for love.

When Luke looked at his girlfriend with those puppy dog eyes, Matthew generally ribbed him, but deep down he wanted the same thing.

CHAPTER 2

After saying his goodbyes and promising to let everyone know about Mimi and Hank's good news, he took off for home. It was a long drive and he looked forward to getting back on his ranch and seeing his family and friends. Matthew was a homebody at heart, but who could blame him?

His ranch was known all over the country. Other ranchers came to visit him from as far away as Oklahoma and Texas on a regular basis. In fact, that was how Hank had met Mimi. He had come to The Triple J Ranch to see how they raised their cattle and what exactly the secret ingredient was for such tender, juicy beef. The two cowboys became friends during that visit, and Hank got himself a bride.

Matthew was fairly outgoing and enjoyed having visitors. If it weren't for his pet project of breeding horses, he'd never have to leave his ranch. Plenty of people visited often enough he didn't want for company or good conversation. Not to mention his large family.

On the long drive home, Matthew thought about all the exciting things his family had done growing up. If he didn't marry and have a large family, at least he'd have a lot of nieces and nephews. He was very confident his brothers and sisters would provide more than enough children to make the Triple J rowdy and full of love.

Maybe he didn't have to marry after all. He could be the fun uncle that all the kids wanted to see. He'd be able to spoil them all rotten and then send them back home once he was ready to do something different. Wasn't that what most grandpas and uncles did?

As he was approaching the turn-off to Beacon Creek, he noticed a large poster on the side of the road. It was propped up as though someone had put it in the perfect place for drivers to notice. The sign read, *Just Hitched*, and there were painted flowers around the edges of the white cardboard that had seen better days. The edges were frayed, and a tire tread ran through the middle of the sign.

"Great, people can't even be bothered with picking up their trash anymore. What's this world coming to if even the Montana highways are covered with litter?" He pulled over and picked up the sign and threw it in the back of his truck. He'd throw it in the burn pile when he got home.

Not wanting to think about the newlywed couple, he looked out in the distance to the Big Sky country that he loved so much. The sun was beginning to set, and the orange and red sky swathed in burnt sienna clouds settled his soul. The distant horizon was dotted with sharp mountaintops that he knew well. Come winter, they'd be covered in fluffy white snow. But today they were brown and green.

Behind him in his rearview mirror, he could still see the mountains he'd driven through not long ago. They were so tall and majestic they stole most of the sky from his view.

Something white ahead caught his attention, and he began to slow down. "No, it couldn't be." He didn't know who he was talking to. Maybe God was listening? Either way, he continued to slow and looked around the sides of the road for a car or another person. There was nothing but the brush interspersed among the fields of hay growing alongside the road.

He stopped behind a woman wearing a tattered wedding dress. It had been white at one time, but now it was covered in dirt and bits of hay or grass. When he stepped out of his truck, the woman turned around and he gasped.

Her hair was a rat's nest, her stare was vacant, and she had blood dripping down the side of her face that had already splattered her once-beautiful dress.

"Are you alright?" He cringed when he heard his careless words. Of course she wasn't alright. The woman looked as though she'd been in an accident and rolled around on the ground before getting back up. "I'm sorry. My name is Matthew Manning. May I help you?"

She continued to stare at him with a vacant expression. The woman just stood there blinking back tears mixed with her blood.

He took a few steps closer to her and put his hands up in a placating gesture. "I won't hurt you," he whispered. "I'm here to help."

She still hadn't spoken to him. And he wondered what had happened to the poor woman. Was that her sign not two miles back on the road that he'd picked up? He hadn't noticed any vehicles or signs of other people on the road. Where was her groom?

"Where's your husband?" he calmly asked. The last thing he wanted to do was to spook the poor filly. But he had to know where the man was. Who knew if he was lying hurt— or worse, in a ditch somewhere along the road?

Without a word, she walked toward him. When she was

only two paces away, her eyes flittered and she fell forward into his arms.

"Whoa. Ma'am? Ma'am?" He didn't want to shake her, but she wasn't moving and he wasn't sure if she was even alive.

Matthew moved the woman in his arms so he could see her face. Her eyes were closed, but her chest was moving. Which meant she was breathing. The poor filly must have fainted in relief at finally seeing help. He looked around and didn't see anything or anyone in the area.

They were only about thirty minutes from Beacon Creek. There were other smaller towns closer, but he didn't think any of them had a clinic. The woman in his arms needed help. With only her best interests at heart, he picked her up and carried her back to his truck.

Once she was laid out on the bench seat in the back of his cab, he used the seat belts to hold her in place. It couldn't have been comfortable for her to have the belts digging into her back, but he didn't know what else to do to keep her safe.

Before he got back in the driver's seat, he felt the pulse at her neck and on her wrist. Her heartbeat seemed strong. Then he noticed the gash on the side of her head and found a clean shirt from his duffel and wiped the blood and dirt away.

Head wounds always bled the worst, but hers had already started to clot. He knew that was a good sign, but it also meant she had been bleeding for a long time. It also explained all the blood on the front of her dress, in her hair, and on her face.

Matthew left the shirt on her head and got into the driver's seat. Using the Bluetooth connection on his truck, he called 911.

"911 operator, what's your emergency?" The woman on

the other side of the phone sounded calm and cool, which was not how he felt at that moment.

"I found a woman in a wedding dress on the side of the road. She's bleeding and unconscious. But there isn't a car or another person around." Matthew explained exactly where he was and where he was taking the bride.

The operator took all his contact information and said she would ensure the Beacon Creek Clinic was ready for his arrival. Then she said she would send a patrol car to look for the woman's car and possibly another person on the side of the road.

With all the area small towns, farms, and ranches, it would be difficult to know where she had come from and who she was. They would have to wait for her to wake up. The 911 operator informed Matthew that there were no missing bride reports and no accidents had been reported on that highway for the past few days.

When he hung up, he hit his steering wheel and sped up. The poor woman did not have anyone looking for her, which meant she could not have been gone long. But what about her groom? She must have just married and been on her way to Bozeman for her honeymoon. Maybe they were going to fly out of Bozeman Yellowstone International Airport and go somewhere tropical for their honeymoon?

He shook his head and refocused on the road in front of him. It would not do any good for him to speculate where the woman was heading before getting into an accident. He had to get her to the doctor…fast.

"Hang on little filly, I'll get you to the doc right away." He looked through his rearview mirror to see the cowgirl lying on his seat, eyes still closed. No more blood had trickled down her face, which was a good thing. At least she would not be losing any more blood before he got her to the clinic.

He did a double take when he noticed the light-blue boots on her feet. Only a cowgirl would wear boots under her wedding dress.

CHAPTER 3

The moment he pulled into the clinic's little driveway, he noticed a stretcher, two nurses, and a doctor waiting patiently for them. One of the nurses he knew—Harper Bensen. *Good*, he thought. At least this little filly would be getting the best care possible in his town.

Before he was even out of his door, the back door had been opened and the nurses were unbuckling the unconscious woman.

"What do you know about her?" Harper asked without even looking at him.

"I found her on the side of the road. She was conscious but didn't seem coherent." Matthew began telling them all of what he had seen and done.

The medical professionals took the unconscious woman into the clinic on a gurney, and he followed behind them. When he tried to follow them into the exam room, Harper put a hand on his shoulder.

"Matthew, you'll have to stay in the waiting room." She eyed him pointedly.

He could feel the tips of his ears burn, and he realized his mistake. "Sorry. Of course." He walked back a few steps before turning around and heading toward the small waiting area that looked more like a doctor's office reception room.

Plastic chairs lined two walls with a side table in the corner and several coffee tables in front of the chairs. On the tables were various horse magazines and one PBR Finals pamphlet.

The white walls and light-cream linoleum floor did not do anything to calm him down. He felt like he was the one waiting for bad news from the doctor. Instead of sitting down, he paced the length of the room and occasionally hit his hat against his thigh.

After what seemed like hours, but was most likely a little over an hour, Harper came out of the exam room. "Matthew, we're going to keep her overnight. You might as well go home."

"Is she alright? Has she woken up yet?" He did not even know her name, but he felt protective of the little filly. If one of his sisters had been in the same predicament, he hoped a local rancher would take responsibility for her. He was going to do no less than what he would expect for his sisters.

"I'm afraid I can't tell you anything about her condition other than to say she has woken up. I'll be staying the night to keep an eye on her, don't worry." She smiled placatingly at the overly large cowboy in her tiny waiting room.

"Can I see her before I leave?" Matthew held his Stetson in front of him with both hands.

When Harper frowned, Matthew feared she would turn him away. "Let me see if she's willing to see you. Wait here." The nurse turned on her heels and headed back behind the door to the mysterious woman in the tattered wedding gown.

He ran a hand down his face and realized he had not shaved since he left the Walton ranch. His mother would have a fit when he returned home with two days' growth on his face.

His back was to the exam room, but he heard footsteps behind him and turned back around. "Well?" He looked at his friend expectantly.

The smile on Harper's face told him all he needed to know. He took several steps forward to follow the nurse into the exam room.

Matthew smiled at the woman, who had been cleaned up and was wearing a hospital gown. She had an IV in her arm with two different bags hanging from the pole and a blood pressure cuff on her left arm. "Good ev'nen,' ma'am." He did not know her name and knew he couldn't address her as *filly*, like he had in his head. Since she was most likely married, *ma'am* was the proper greeting.

"Claire, this is the cowboy who saved you from the side of the road. Matthew Manning, let me introduce you to Claire Brown." Harper stood on the other side of Claire's bed, smiling at the two before she turned to look at the monitor on the bedside table.

"Mr. Manning, thank you so much for helping me." She looked at him curiously, almost as though she was trying to place him but could not.

"Mrs. Brown, I'm glad I came along when I did. Do you know where your husband is?" He was worried about the fact that she was all alone on the side of the road.

Since he had seen the *Just Hitched* sign, he was confident their car was somewhere along the road—it had to be. He supposed it was possible she had walked miles before he had found her. The sign could have floated on the breeze, or maybe even on the front of a car before landing where it did. Maybe her accident happened in the mountains? He would have to tell the sheriff what he thought when he was done here.

The confusion on her face had him worried.

"I…" She put a hand to her head and winced. "I'm sorry, but I don't remember." She looked to Harper with pleading eyes.

"Can I tell him?" Harper was a stickler for following HIPAA guidelines. She would never divulge anyone's medical information without their express permission.

Claire nodded.

Harper took a deep breath. "Claire has amnesia. The head wound probably caused it. The doctor thinks she'll get her memory back soon. But for now, she has no idea who she is or what happened."

Creases formed along Matthew's brow, and he considered the woman's situation. "Then how do you know her name? She didn't have a purse—I looked."

The nurse nodded and looked to the tiny cupboard in the room. "Inside her gown was her name."

"Ah. Okay." Matthew turned his gaze back to Claire. "Mrs. Brown…"

She held up a hand. "Please, call me Claire. Mrs. Brown doesn't feel right."

If she had just married, he doubted her subconscious would accept her new name. He was happy to oblige. "Claire, if there is anythin' I can do to help, all you have to do is ask. I'm at your disposal."

When the woman in the bed smiled, he noticed her green eyes for the first time and the little dimple on her right cheek. Even though her blonde hair was still a mess, she was beautiful.

He had to shake his head and remind himself he should

not be admiring another man's wife. And certainly not one in a hospital bed with amnesia.

"Thank you, Mr. Manning. I appreciate it."

"Please, call me Matthew." He gripped the brim of his hat and had to practically bite his tongue to keep from grinning at the filly in front of him.

The door behind him opened, and he turned around to see the local sheriff walk in.

"Howdy, ma'am. I'm Sheriff Roscoe." He tipped his head toward Claire.

"My name is Claire. Nice to meet you, Sheriff. Do you have any news?" She turned hopeful eyes on the lawman who had entered her room and now stood next to Matthew. While the sheriff was tall and broad-shouldered, he did not compare to Matthew's height.

She was not sure, but she guessed Matthew to be at least six feet tall, probably more. His broad shoulders made the sheriff's look like a young boy's, even though the man was probably in his late forties or early fifties.

The sheriff cleared his throat. "I'm sorry, but no news yet. The state police are still searching the highway and any side roads in the area. Can you tell me where you were coming from or going to? I understand you were wearing a wedding dress?"

Claire took a deep breath before informing the sheriff she could not remember anything.

"The only reason we know her name is because it was sewn into her dress," Matthew added.

"Well, that doesn't necessarily mean that you are Claire Brown. You could be wearing a secondhand dress." The sheriff could not have shocked Claire more if he had thrown a bucket of cold water on her.

"But, that... No. I wouldn't wear a used dress. Not for my

wedding." Claire was adamant about it. She did not know why, but she was confident the dress was hers.

"What else do you remember about your dress?" Harper had a clipboard in her hands with a pen and was writing something down.

"Huh? That's strange." Confusion was written all over Claire's face. "How do I know it's my dress?"

"This is normal, Claire." The heart monitor next to the patient was starting to beep louder, and Harper looked at it and furrowed her brow. "Just relax. Don't worry about it."

"I don't know anything else. Why can't I remember?" Claire pounded her left hand on the bed beside her, and the pulse monitor on her finger flew off and hit the floor.

Harper bent down to pick it up. When she calmly put it back on Claire's finger, she smiled at her patient. "Please, Claire. Calm down. You heard the doctor. Memories will come back to you one at a time very slowly. It's best not to stress over them. Let them come at their own pace." Harper glanced at the display next to her and smiled. "That's it. Just relax and don't worry. We'll take good care of you."

After Harper placed the clipboard on the end of the hospital bed, she turned her gaze to Matthew. "I'm sorry, but you're going to have to leave now. She needs rest. You can come back tomorrow and visit if you like."

Nodding, Matthew smiled at Claire. "I'll be back first thing tomorrow mornin'. Nurse Harper knows how to reach me if you need anythin' at all." He turned to leave, but stopped. "Sheriff, I'll be out in the waitin' room."

The sheriff nodded.

Once Matthew left the room, the sheriff turned his attention back on the patient in front of him. "Mrs. Brown, is there anything else you can tell me about what happened, or where you're from?"

She shook her head. "Please, call me Claire." She furrowed her brow and continued, "Mrs. Brown doesn't feel right." Her heart monitor began beeping again, and she sighed.

Nurse Harper put a calming hand on her patient's shoulder. "Claire, there's no need to stress over it. Go with your gut feeling. In your situation, that's usually what's correct."

Claire looked at her hand. "Where's my wedding ring?" She worried at her bottom lip. "Something feels off about it. It's like there's something there, something that I know, but I just can't reach it." With sadness in her eyes, she looked up to Harper. "Why can't I reach the memory that's begging me to come out?"

Harper softened her eyes and smiled at her charge. "Claire, this is just part of the process for remembering. You're going to feel like this a lot. It's best to just relax and let the memories come when they're ready."

When the door opened, all eyes turned to the doctor as he walked in. "Sheriff, I'm afraid I'm going to have to ask you to leave now. The mobile CT scanner has arrived and we need to scan Claire's brain, just to be on the safe side."

"Of course. I'll be back in the morning to check on your patient. Hopefully we'll have more news then." Sheriff Roscoe turned back to Claire. "Ma'am, I'm glad to see you're doin' alright. Dr. Montgomery here will take good care of you."

Claire only hoped the sheriff was right.

CHAPTER 4

The entire ride home, Matthew could not help but think about the bride he'd found along the side of the road. She had been so dirty, and with the blood on her head and dress he worried about what had happened to her. He was also concerned about her groom. As he drove home, he prayed for the safety of her missing husband.

The last thing Claire needed was to find out her new husband had died, and she could not even remember him.

By the time he returned home, his entire family was awaiting his return. It seemed Beacon Creek's gossip mill, aka the Diner Divas, had been hard at work while he was in the clinic waiting to hear about Claire.

"Oh, Matthew, is it true?" his mother, Judith Manning, asked as she ushered her oldest son inside the ranch house.

He hugged his mother before looking to all the expectant eyes in the room. "Well, I don't rightly know what you've heard, but I did find a woman on the side of the road and took her into the clinic."

Caleb Manning, Matthew's father, rubbed a hand down

his face. "I've been prayin' for her from the moment your ma told me the town gossip. How is she?"

Matthew led his family into the kitchen, where he went straight to the coffee pot and sighed. "Bless you. I've needed a good cup of joe ever since I set eyes on Claire."

Luke's brow furrowed, and he was about to ask who Claire was when Matthew turned around with a cup of black coffee in hand.

"Claire's her name." He took a long gulp of the hot drink, and his shoulders relaxed. "She was in a filthy weddin' dress walkin' alon' the side of the road when I stopped to help to her." Matthew continued to tell them the story of the little filly he had rescued once everyone sat around the kitchen table.

Mark scratched behind his ear. "If she's got amnesia, how is it ya know her name?"

"It was sewn into her weddin' dress." Matthew shrugged. He did not know much about weddings or dresses, but he figured that if the hospital knew to look in her dress for a name, it must be a normal thing.

Mrs. Manning's eyes widened. "She must have had a custom dress made if her name was sewn into it. Or it was designer. That's not normal for an off-the-rack dress."

Elizabeth Hayes, Matthew's sister who had recently married, nodded. "I didn't put my name in my dress since it was a simple gown I found in a bridal store in Bozeman."

"Well, either way she's goin' t' be fine." He laughed ruefully. "If you don't count her amnesia."

Mrs. Manning tsk'd. "That will go away. She'll eventually remember who she is. It's not uncommon to have amnesia from a head injury. I just wish we knew how she was injured and where her car is."

"And where her husband is," Elizabeth added.

Everyone around the table nodded, and no one spoke for a few minutes.

"I have some stew in the ice box if you're hungry, Matthew." Mrs. Manning loved to feed her family. Especially during difficult situations. She believed that, other than prayer, the next best thing to mending the heart was a full stomach.

"Thanks, Ma. I could actually use somethin' before headin' to bed. I need to get up early to get chores done and then I'm headin' into the clinic to check on Claire." It was approaching the eight o'clock hour, and thanks to the long day he was already yawning. Matthew stood up and went to his mother.

She was shorter than his six feet, three inches, so he leaned down to buss her cheek with a quick kiss. Mrs. Manning batted him away, but smiled at her eldest son before turning to the refrigerator to grab some stew to heat up for him.

THE NEXT MORNING came bright and earlier than Matthew had wanted. Normally after a long trip he let himself sleep in, but today he could not. He had too many responsibilities at the ranch to take care of before he could leave to head into town.

The moment the sun was up, he downed a quick cup of coffee and headed out to feed the horses. He had agreed with his brothers the night before that they would take care of the cattle and ride the fence line to check for any breaks. But his responsibility was to the horses first.

Once they were fed, watered, and checked on, he went into the house for a quick breakfast. Then he showered and headed out to the Beacon Creek Clinic to check on his filly.

He was not sure when he began to think of Claire as his filly, but he did. Maybe it was because she was so vulnerable at the moment and there were not any family or friends to take care of her. Since he was the one who had found her, he believed it was his responsibility to care for the woman until her family was located. Even if she was married.

While Claire was beautiful, he did not think of her in a romantic way. He did not pity her, but he was concerned for her well-being. Thoughts of what would happen if Chloe was in Claire's situation kept running through his mind.

Chloe was Elizabeth's twin, and she lived in Frenchtown. While she had been there for a little while now and had made friends, he still worried for her safety. Especially after seeing what happened with Claire. As the oldest Manning child, Matthew had always felt responsible for all six of his siblings. Even though his parents were still alive and took great care of the entire family, he was still the oldest brother.

When Matthew arrived at the clinic, he drew himself out of his thoughts about how to protect his siblings while also caring for the new cowgirl in town. Until her family was located, he knew what he had to do.

The clinic was small; it only had a dozen hospital beds, more for minor injuries and illnesses. A few years back they got their own X-ray machine. The next year they had set up the ability to bring in a mobile CAT scan or MRI machine as necessary. While they did have good doctors, they were not equipped to handle anything major. With Bozeman only a little over thirty minutes away, they did not have the need for more.

Most injuries that happened on the local ranches or farms were easily handled at their own clinic. If it was major, then the local doctors could help while the patient was transported to the Bozeman hospital. Only once in the past ten years had an injury been so bad that Beacon Creek needed to Life Flight anyone out. He was confident Claire would get the best possible medical care while she was there.

By the time Matthew reached Claire's room, she was sitting up eating a late breakfast.

"Hi. How ya feelin' today?" Matthew smiled at the woman before he entered the open door to her room.

Claire put down her fork and motioned for him to sit next to her as she pushed the rolling tray out of her way. "I'm feeling much better this morning."

"I'm very happy to hear that." He took his hat in his hand and turned it around. "Do you remember anythin' yet?" While Matthew did not want to push her or cause her any more pain, he was curious.

His sister, Elizabeth, was a vet. Even though she only worked on animals, she did have a medical background. While he ate his stew the night before, she told him a little bit about amnesia and said a good night's sleep might bring her memory back, or it could be weeks before Claire remembered anything.

The important thing was that she was receiving the best care possible.

Claire winced. "No, nothing yet." The woman sighed and looked at her folded hands in her lap.

"How was breakfast? Looks like you ate most of it." Matthew was not really sure what to talk about. Since she had lost her memory, it was not like he could ask her what she did for a living, or where she was from.

She smiled. "It was surprisingly good. I may not have my memory back yet, but something tells me hospital food isn't supposed to be this good."

A chuckle escaped Matthew before he realized it. This was not exactly a laughing matter, but she was right. "Yeah, we don't have a hospital kitchen here. Rosie's Diner prepares meals for any patients who might stay overnight."

"Wow, that was a diner breakfast? It tasted too healthy. I think it was an egg white omelet with veggies and ham. And a side of sliced tomatoes." Her hand covered her full stomach, and she wondered what she would be served for lunch.

"Darn tootin' it's healthy and delicious. Rosie has been caterin' to the various health needs of our community for years. She started a gluten-free menu before the fruits out west said it was cool." He chortled, remembering when the health food options began popping up on the menu and began to miss his friends from Wyoming.

When Mimi Harper first came home from college, she had learned that she was sensitive to gluten and Rosie started making up different concoctions for her. After that, people started to see the differences in Mimi and quite a few began asking for the same things the recent college graduate ate.

Even his sisters and their friends started cutting gluten from their diet wherever they could.

"The bread tasted a little bit different, but it was good." Claire looked to her plate and realized she had cleaned almost the entire thing. She wondered if that was normal for her or not. She looked to be in good shape and not overweight. How did she keep her figure?

If she continued to eat so much, she doubted she would stay skinny, especially if she was stuck in the hospital bed for more than a day. She had the feeling she was an active sort. Her time in the hospital bed had already been too much, she feared. Her legs itched to get out and stretch.

"Maybe I run marathons?" The whisper blurted out, and she blinked her eyes a few times.

"Huh? You run marathons? Is that a memory coming

back?" Matthew hoped she would start remembering. The poor filly's family must be worried sick by now.

She shrugged. "I don't know. But sitting here in bed so long has me antsy. My legs are begging me to get out and do something." Claire tilted her head to the right, and a small smile lifted the corner of her lips up.

"I don't blame you. There's no way I could stay cooped up in the hospital for long. When will you be released?"

At that moment, the doctor walked in. "If she had a place to go, I'd release her today." Doctor Montgomery shook Matthew's hand and smiled at his patient.

"She can come out to our ranch. I know my ma would be happy to have her stay with us." This was exactly the opening Matthew needed to ensure he was able to take care of the bride until her family was located.

Claire's eyes widened, and her mouth opened. "But you don't even know me, do you? Why would you offer to help me like this?"

Matthew stood up taller and smiled at the woman. "Because I have two sisters. If one of them were in your boots, I'd hope a nice family would look out for them until we found 'em."

"You do have a nice ranch with plenty of room." The doctor held Claire's chart in his hands. "Claire, if you agree, then I'd be happy to release you to the care of the Manning family. Nurse Harper is good friends with them, and I'm sure she'll be happy to come out to take vitals and check on you as needed."

"Really?" Claire was not sure what to make of this offer. Her soul yearned to get out of the hospital, and a still-small voice within told her to trust Matthew. If the doctor trusted the Mannings, shouldn't that be enough? She mulled over the prospect for a few second before nodding. "Thank you, Matthew. That would be wonderful."

A lightness floated over Matthew, and he smiled at Claire before turning to the doctor. "Okay, what do we need to do to help her? Are there any restrictions we should be aware of?"

"I want her to take it easy for the next few days. Claire didn't have a concussion, so I don't rightly know what caused her memory loss. The scans are all clear, but she does have a nasty bump on her head." The doctor looked between the two.

"How long before she can ride a horse?" Matthew wanted to take her out for a ride. A bride who wore cowboy boots under her wedding dress was most definitely a horse woman. He hoped it might jog her memory if riding was a regular activity for her.

While he did not recognize her, she could be a rodeo rider, or maybe a horse trainer? If he was lucky, she was a horse breeder. Being around horses just might help to jog her memory.

"At least three days. Then just be sure to monitor her and don't ride too hard. Take it easy and see how she feels. I think Claire will be able to tell you if she needs to take a break or if it's alright to keep going." The doctor spoke with Matthew as though he was her caretaker and the patient were not even in the room.

"Uh, excuse me." Claire put her hand up. "I'm right here. Don't you think I'm the one who needs to know this information?" She rolled her eyes and thought, *Men. Silly creatures.*

Matthew chuckled. He liked her spunk.

The doctor cleared his throat. "Of course, Claire. Please forgive me. It's just that Matthew will be responsible for your care. I know you're capable of taking care of yourself, but if you want me to release you, I have to explain to him"—he pointed to the cowboy—"all your medical needs."

Claire shook her head and sighed. She may not remember her life, but one thing was clear to her: she was not a shrinking violet. "I think it's more important that *I* understand how to care for myself." She raised an eyebrow before continuing. "Don't you think?"

Dr. Montgomery nodded. "Of course. I'll be sure to have the nurse print out your instructions along with the number to my service in case you have any questions. I'd like to see you back here in five days for a follow-up. Nurse Harper will be by to check on you tomorrow afternoon. Will that work?" He looked between patient and caregiver.

They both nodded.

"Alright, then I'll send a nurse back in here to help you dress and take your IV out while I finish up the paperwork." He left the room with the door open.

"You're goin' ta love my ranch." Matthew's excitement shone through his eyes. He loved to show off the Triple J Ranch and could not wait to take Claire for a ride.

Happiness bubbled up in Claire's chest and butterflies scurried through her stomach. She was not sure if she was excited to be leaving the clinic or to be heading to Matthew's ranch. Maybe a little bit of both. "Something tells me I like ranches." She put a finger to her chin. "And I think horses." She beamed.

Matthew slapped his hands together. "Fantastic! Just as soon as the doc allows it, I'll take ya ridin'."

Before Claire had a chance to answer, Harper walked into the room. "I see you're going to get the Manning family treatment. Lucky you." She looked between the two people in the room, then smiled. "And lucky me. I think you should expect me around five o'clock every night to check on you." Harper winked at Matthew.

He chuckled. "Duly noted. I'll be sure ta have an extra place settin' for ya each night."

Confusion covered Claire's face.

"Oh, Harper enjoys havin' supper at our place," Matthew said. "I'm sure we'll be grillin' up quite a few steaks this week."

Harper nodded and licked her lips. "You haven't had barbecue until you've had a Manning barbecue. Their beef is the best in the country, and Matthew makes a mean sauce."

Even though she had recently had breakfast, Claire's stomach rumbled, and she could feel heat creep up her cheeks. "I guess that means I like steak?"

Claire tried to laugh off her embarrassment. Matthew and Harper laughed with her.

"Alright, Matthew. I'll need you to leave the room while I get Claire ready to leave the clinic." Harper pointed to the door.

Matthew closed the door behind him when he left and went to sit out in the small waiting room.

After the door closed, Claire looked to Harper. "I don't have anything other than that tattered wedding gown. What am I supposed to wear?"

"Here." In Harper's hands was a set of scrubs and a pair of slip-on tennis shoes.

Claire took the offered clothes and furrowed her brow. "Are these yours?" She looked the nurse up and down and realized that while they were close in size, Claire was smaller in stature than Harper. These clothes would be too big for her.

Harper held up a hand. "I realize they might not fit well, but they are comfortable. I'll work on finding something better for you and bring it out tonight when I come to check on you."

"You mean, when you come for supper?" Claire smirked.

With a finger on her chin, Harper thought for a moment. "Sure, I suppose I could stay for supper tonight." The grin on her face caused Claire to laugh lightly and shake her head.

"Alright, but I think I'll want to wear my boots." Claire eyed the lavender scrub pants and the matching floral scrub top and realized she was going to clash something awful with her turquoise boots. But a part of her felt comfort when she thought about her boots. They were the only thing that tied her to her past.

A past she wanted desperately to remember.

CHAPTER 5

Matthew could not help the giant smile across his face when he saw Claire's reaction.

They had just pulled up to the front of his ranch home and her face shone with a huge smile and wide eyes when she stepped out of his truck and took in the house.

"This is beautiful. You live here?" Claire could not believe she was going to be staying in such a large ranch home. And it was a home. With the cozy seats and cushions on the covered porch and the large porch swing to the side, she knew right away she was going to enjoy her stay here.

Nights spent sitting on the porch drinking iced tea and watching as the sun set sounded like something she was accustomed to. A pain shot through her temple, and she stopped in her tracks. Claire put a hand to her head and began to massage her pounding temple.

"Are you alright?" Matthew stepped up next to her and took her free elbow. He helped her up the steps and set her down on the wooden chair next to the front door.

"You're here…" Mrs. Manning's smile diminished when she saw the worry on her son's face. "What's wrong?"

He looked up to his mother and then back down to his charge. "Claire's in pain." Matthew took her free hand in his and squeezed it lightly. "What's wrong?"

Claire winced and tried to shake her head, but it only made the pain worse. "I'm not sure."

"Ma, can you get her two Advil liquid gels? The doc said she could take them if she was in pain." He did not take his eyes off Claire, and he worried he'd be taking her back to the clinic before he even got her inside his house.

"I'll be right back with a glass of water, too." Mrs. Manning turned around and went right back inside to her bathroom where she kept a bottle of pain reliever in her medicine cabinet.

"Is there anythin' I can do to help?" Matthew did not know what else to do. Maybe he should call Harper and ask her. If Claire's headache did not dissipate soon, he would.

"No, just give me a moment." Claire's breathing was ragged, and she squeezed her eyes to block out the light. At the same time, she was trying to grasp the memory that had made a few attempts to come through. Something about this porch had triggered a faint picture in her mind. She could see an older woman smiling and rocking in a wooden chair on a porch similar to this one, but it would not stick. It kept coming and going.

The more she tried to grab ahold of it, the more intense the pain became. She pulled her hand out of Matthew's and put it to her other temple and began to rub. As the memory faded, so too did the pain until both were just a wisp of a ghost.

Mrs. Manning came out with a glass of water and two greenish-blue liquid gels in her hand. "Here sweetie, take these with the water." She handed the pills to Claire, and the young woman put them in her mouth before taking the glass of water.

Once the pills were down and Claire finished the water, she looked up into the worried faces of her rescuer and his mother. "Thank you."

"Should I call the doctor?" Matthew asked, worry lines creasing his forehead.

"No, the doctor warned me I might get these headaches." She leaned back in the chair and sighed. "A memory was starting to surface, and I think I tried to force it out."

Matthew ran a hand through his hair and sighed heavily. "Yeah, Harper told me that you needed to let the memories come on their own. You can't force 'em."

"Ugh, I know. It's just so frustrating to not know who I am. And to have glimpses of memories tugging at me to call them forth is just too much." Claire knew what she was doing was wrong, but she could not help herself. The sooner she got her memory back, the sooner she could figure out what had happened to her supposed groom.

Again, something felt off. She was in a wedding gown but did not have a ring on her finger. And the last name "Brown" caused anxiety to well up in her gut—not happiness, like it should. She wondered if they had been attacked and her attackers took her wedding ring and her husband? If the sheriff had not found signs of her car or groom, that had to be it, right?

But this was not the old wild west. Highwaymen did not sneak up on unsuspecting couples and kidnap them and steal from them anymore. Did they? She did have amnesia, but other than her life, she felt as though her memory was fine. She knew what year it was and who the president was. She just did not know who *she* was.

The turquoise boots on her feet were comfortable, as

though she had worn them in, so she knew that her suspected love of horses had to mean she lived on a ranch somewhere. She most likely had her own horse, but she could not remember it.

It was also possible that she just loved horses and was a wannabe cowgirl.

Matthew stood up and gave Claire a small smile. "Let me introduce you to my mother, properly." He looked to his mother. "Ma, this is Claire Brown, the woman I told you about." He turned to Claire. "Claire, this is my mother, Judith Manning."

Claire stood up and smiled at the woman who exuded warmth and welcome. "Thank you so much for allowing me to convalesce here instead of the clinic. I really do appreciate it." She put her hand out to shake, but Judith stepped into her personal space instead.

Judith wrapped Claire in her arms and said, "Don't say a thing. It's our pleasure to help you." She released Claire and took a step back. Even with lines around her eyes and a few around her mouth, the woman still looked youthful and beautiful.

Claire could not believe this was the mother of seven children. While the auburn-haired cowgirl wearing Wranglers, brown boots, and a pink-checkered blouse had to be at least fifty-five, the woman looked like she was still in her late thirties, possibly early forties. She thought ranch life was tough on people, but maybe this ranch was good for Mrs. Manning? Or she just had good genes.

Claire could only hope when she was older, she would look as good as Mrs. Manning.

"Please, come on in. I bet you're starved. Did you get much for breakfast today?" Mrs. Manning opened the door and led the two into her kitchen.

"Actually, I had a large breakfast. But if you have some coffee, that would be wonderful." The idea of coffee just came to Claire as though it was something she did every day. Was it? She could not be sure, but when she thought about how she wanted it, she knew it must be how she normally started her day.

"How do you like your coffee?" Mrs. Manning stood at the counter with a cup of black coffee in hand and waited for Claire's response.

"With two creams and one Stevia In The Raw, please." Before Claire took a seat at the table, Matthew snorted and shook his head. "What?" She looked at the cowboy in confusion.

"We don't have fancy sugar here. It's either real sugar or Sweet 'n' Low." He took a seat next to her.

"Huh, I guess that works too, right?" Claire looked to her hostess and moved a stray strand of hair out of her face.

If she could remember how she liked her coffee, then maybe her memory would come back quickly. Matthew really hoped it was so. He could not imagine being in her boots. His eyes slid down to under the table when he thought about her boots, and he smirked. They really did not go well with purple scrubs.

"Ma, do we have any clothes that might fit Claire?" He smiled at his mother when she brought him his cup of black coffee.

Mrs. Manning looked at Claire and considered what size the girl might be. She was smaller than her own daughters, so those clothes would not work. But she had collected quite a few different sizes for the next time they went into Bozeman to help the homeless women. "I think I might have something. I'll go look." She smiled at the two sitting at her table drinking their coffee, and she left.

"You remembered how you like your coffee? Did that cause a headache?" He winced when he imagined how it might hurt Claire to recall such a simple memory and hoped she was not in any more pain.

She shook her head. "Actually, the idea just came out. The doctor told me that if I didn't think about things, only acted, then bits and pieces would come back to me." She took a sip of the hot liquid and sighed. "This is really good, even without stevia." She chuckled.

Matthew could not help but join her. It reminded him of all the times he had argued with his high school girlfriend over Coke and Pepsi. He was a Coke man, and she loved Diet Pepsi. He never could understand why she drank the stuff, it tasted so sugary. Then he wondered which Claire would prefer.

"Coke or Pepsi?" he blurted out.

She raised her brows and turned her head to look at him. "Hmm?"

"Which do you prefer? Don't think, just answer."

"Diet Coke, I think?" Her lips quirked.

Matthew found himself staring at her plump lips and scolded himself for looking at a married woman's mouth. She was recently married, probably in just the past day or two. He had no business looking at her lips or feeling any stirrings whatsoever when he did.

"What do you drink?" she asked, oblivious to his internal battle to keep his eyes off her.

Without thinking, he replied, "Coke, of course. Most of Beacon Creek serves Coke products. It's a good thing that's what you like, as our house refuses to carry anything Pepsi." He looked down at his mug of coffee and smiled.

"Then I guess I ended up in the right place." She nodded at him.

"Here, I have a box of clothes that might fit you." Mrs. Manning walked into the room carrying a large box that wobbled in her arms.

Matthew stood up immediately. "Here, Ma. Let me." He took the box from her arms and set it down on the table.

"Nothing in here would be considered fashionable, but you might find something comfortable that could match your fancy boots." Mrs. Manning pointed to Claire's feet.

Claire could feel her cheeks warm at the attention. "They're all I've got of my past, and they're rather comfortable." She shrugged and kept her eyes on the clothes in the box.

Claire stood up and began rummaging through. When she looked at the tags, she realized she did not even know her own size. "I don't know if they'll fit. Do you mind if I take them to a room to try on later?" She yawned and covered her mouth.

"Oh, where are my manners? Of course, you're probably tired after checking out of the hospital. Why don't I take you to the guest room and you lay down for a nap? I'll come and wake you when lunch is ready." Mrs. Manning tried to lift the box off the table, but Matthew put a hand out to stop her and he took it instead.

After Claire had napped and changed clothes, she felt like a different woman. Her headache was gone. Well, mostly gone. She only had a faint echo of pain left in the back of her head. With a good night's rest, she figured it would be fully gone come morning. She still had a few body aches, but nothing major. Maybe she would take a long, hot bath before bed that night.

What she hadn't expected was to find so many different clothes that fit her, and were cute. Even though she could not remember her name from Adam, she did think she must have liked fashion at least a little bit. As she rummaged through the box, her mind criticized the clothes and she had to mentally kick herself for being so ungrateful. There were three full outfits that fit and did not look half-bad. No matter what, it was better than scrubs. There was even a long, soft cashmere-feeling sweater that went down to her knees. The turquoise and gray flourishes through the pattern looked really nice with her boots.

Claire had read the tag; it was not cashmere, but it was very soft and pretty. Probably the best item in the box. She could not believe her luck to get something so feminine from a box of donated clothes. It fit her so well that she was going to have to make sure she kept this one item when she got her memory back. Even if that meant replacing something from her own wardrobe with it.

A knock sounded on her door as she finished brushing her long, blonde hair. "Come on in."

The door squeaked open, and Mrs. Manning's head peeked in. "I think I'll have Matthew oil this door before supper."

Claire chuckled. "Yeah, it's a bit noisy, isn't it?"

"Are you ready for some lunch? I saved you a plate. We made steak sandwiches."

"How late is it?" Claire looked over her shoulder at the clock on the bedside table and gasped. "I'm sorry, I didn't realize it was already two in the afternoon."

Mrs. Manning walked into the room. "Don't worry a thing. I knew you needed sleep." She took something out of her pocket and handed it to Claire. "I also knew you might like a watch to wear."

"Thank you." Claire took the Timex watch with a brown leather band and instinctively put it on her left wrist. "At least

I know I normally wear a watch and am right-handed." She smirked.

A smile spread across Mrs. Manning's face. "Dear, I think you know more than you realize."

Lines formed between Claire's eyes, and she tilted her head to the left. "What do you mean?"

Her hostess pointed to the clothes Claire had on. "I think you know what fashion taste you have. And that you have a love for turquoise."

Claire's face brightened with her smile, and she ran a hand down the soft fibers of the long sweater she wore. "I guess so. I saw this peeking out from the bottom of the box and pulled it out right away. Before I even chose anything else, I knew I had to have this sweater."

"See, that's something you didn't know before you went to sleep." The motherly rancher rubbed Claire's arm warmly and backed up toward the door. "Should I warm up the sandwich for you? And what would you like to drink?"

She nodded. "Yes, please. What do you have to drink?"

"Coffee, tea, Coke, Diet Coke, and Dr. Pepper," Mrs. Manning called out as they walked out of Claire's room and toward the kitchen.

"Do you have sweet tea?"

Mrs. Manning nodded. "See, another clue as to who you are. Only those who normally drink sweet tea would ask for it."

Claire's light laugh echoed off the wall of the kitchen as she entered it, and Matthew's heart pounded hard in his chest. He was going to have to get a hold on his emotions. The filly was married, and he had no right to feel any sort of attraction toward her. He shook his head and thought about the fence line he had to still examine.

"What's that scowl for?" Claire stopped next to Matthew

and looked up, wondering what had caused his brows to furrow and why he had a grimace on his handsome face.

"What?" He shook his head. "Hm? Oh, we've been havin' some issues with the neighbor's bull getting into our pastures. I was thinkin' about the last time this happened and hopin' we weren't in for another gang of cattle rustlers."

"Cattle rustlers? Really?" With eyes as wide as saucers, Claire took two steps back.

Matthew grunted. "No need to worry. I'm sure we just have a broken fence line. The old bull has a thing for a few of our cows and he's been coming into our pasture for years." He rubbed his chin. "That ol' bull always finds the weak spots in our fence line and breaks it."

Claire laughed. "Sounds like someone might be in love." She waggled her brows.

Matthew and Mrs. Manning both laughed.

"Yup, something like that." He pulled a chair back for Claire to sit.

Butterflies swarmed her stomach as though they were going to burst forth, and Claire blinked back a few tears, hoping no one saw the shimmering pools in her eyes. For a brief moment, she felt as though this was a first for her. Surely it could not be. Could it? Whoever she was married to, or engaged to, had to have pulled back a chair for her. Or her father, or brother? She had no clue, but something about this one simple action from a relative stranger made Claire wonder what the men in her life were really like.

A slight chill went down her arms as she sat down and tightened the sweater around herself as though it was a cocoon to protect against a bad memory hanging slightly on the edges of her memory. She wanted to pull it in, but knew that was the wrong thing to do.

And besides, it felt like it might have been something she did not want to remember.

Mrs. Manning put a tall glass of sweet tea and ice in front of Claire, and she sipped it.

"Are you cold?" Matthew looked at Claire with worry in his eyes. She had on a sweater and it was late spring, almost summer. He thought it was too hot to be wearing a sweater during the day. The nights were cool enough for a sweater, but not the day. At least, not today.

"Huh?" Claire looked down. "Oh, no. I just liked the feel of the sweater." She took it off when she realized the chill had left her body and she was beginning to warm up. She may not be able to wear it all day as she hoped, but it would come in handy at times.

"How ya feelin'? Any better than earlier?" Matthew took the seat across from Claire and worried about her health. He had hoped the nap would rejuvenate her, but the dark spots beneath her eyes said she still wasn't feeling right.

"I'm much better. The headache is almost gone." She smiled at Matthew and took a closer look at his face.

He was tanned from working out in the sun, and she could see from the laugh lines forming around his mouth that he was a happy person. He was also quite handsome. Not that she was interested in him—she was married, after all. Wasn't she? A pang hit her hard at the thought of being married to another man, but she did not understand it.

Matthew frowned. "Claire, what's wrong?"

"Hmm? Nothing. Why?" She tilted her head and looked deeper into his eyes and felt something flutter in her stomach. She told herself to knock it off. A married woman did not have feelings for another man, not even a small attraction. It did not matter that any woman would find Matthew Manning handsome; she could not think of him that way.

"You're frowning. Are you in pain?" He took her hand from the table and held it.

Claire blinked a few times and put a smile in place, forced at it was. "No, no. I'm fine. Please, don't worry about me."

Mrs. Manning stood off to the side, watching her son and the beautiful woman at the table. She worried for her son, and the woman. If she was married like everyone assumed, then what she was watching might end up hurting Matthew in the end. She cleared her throat. "Claire, what would you like on your sandwich? Mustard and mayonnaise? Or something else?"

The cowgirl's cheeks flamed hot, and she pulled her hand back and set it in her lap. She was not sure what she was doing, and the fact that Mrs. Manning was watching her unnerved her to no end. "How about barbecue sauce?"

Matthew's left eyebrow arched. "Do you love barbecue?"

Claire shrugged. "Who doesn't?"

When both Mannings chuckled, the tension in the room eased and she felt her shoulders relax.

"Exactly!" Matthew crooned.

The sandwich that Mrs. Manning set in front of Claire was larger than anything she expected. It was on a sub roll that had to be at least eight inches long, with so much meat and sauce dripping from all around the edges that she did not think she'd be able to get it in her mouth.

"Do you have a knife and fork?" Claire chuckled. "This thing is bigger than I am."

Mrs. Manning had already planned on giving her utensils. While the men of the house had no problem eating the sandwich with their hands, she always used a knife and fork to eat the giant sandwich. "Here ya go, dear." She set the silverware down to Claire's right and moved away with a smirk on her face.

"Thank you." Claire beamed at her hostess.

Matthew sat quietly watching as Claire cut into her steak sandwich. He was curious what she would think of the flavor and texture.

Sometimes they used sharp cheddar cheese for the sandwiches, and sometimes swiss. But this time there was not any cheese, just lots and lots of sauce. Sauce he had made from scratch.

Her eyes rolled to the back of her head and she moaned the moment she closed her mouth around her first bite of heaven. "Mmmm." She slowly chewed the tender and rich meat wrapped in a tangy sourdough bread. After she swallowed, she wiped her mouth of the dripping mess she had made and smiled.

"This is the best sandwich I've ever had." Claire laughed. "Or at least, the best sandwich I can remember ever tasting."

Matthew chuckled. "I think there's a compliment in there somewhere?"

His mother stood behind him with a hand on his shoulder. "I'd say there is."

Claire nodded, not wanting to talk any more. She only wanted the spicy sauce-covered tender beef back in her mouth. As she continued to eat, she wondered if Mrs. Manning had made the sourdough bread from scratch, or if she had bought the rolls from a bakery in town. One thing was for sure, she was on her way to gaining weight while she waited for her memory to return, and she did not care.

Just as long as all the food tasted this good.

CHAPTER 6

"Harper! It's so good to see you again. Come on in. Supper's ready." Mrs. Manning hugged Harper and ushered her inside to the kitchen where everyone sat, waiting for dinner to be served.

"Sorry I'm so late. We had a last-minute patient. It seems Mr. Johnson's bull wasn't too happy with him today." Harper raised a brow and looked to Matthew.

Matthew held his hands up. "Hey, I didn't do anythin'."

She put a hand on her hip. "It seems his bull hasn't had any time with his girlfriends lately. Someone's been fixin' fences like crazy."

Everyone in the room chuckled, and Claire looked around in confusion. She wondered why they would laugh at a man who was injured by his own bull, but didn't say anything.

Matthew noticed Claire's furrowed brow. "The Johnsons have a bull, like we said earlier, who's sweet on some of our cows. Lately we've worked extra hard to keep the fences between our pastures solid, keeping that ol' bull away from our cows."

"But is it so bad if the bull visits your cows?" Claire knew something was in her head about this all, but she just could not pull up the memory. The second she tried, a pain shot through her eyes and she winced.

"Hey, are you alright?" Harper immediately went to Claire's side. "Did you just try to access a memory?"

Claire nodded. "I'm fine. It's going away." She took a cleansing breath and smiled at everyone, not wanting them to worry about her.

"I hope Mr. Johnson is alright?" Mrs. Manning decided to change the subject. She knew Claire did not want all eyes on her, especially when they were all worried.

"Yes, it was just a bruise and scratch on his left arm. He only needed five stitches. It was not even from the bull. He ran when it charged and he hit his hand against a wooden fence post that had seen better days." Harper shrugged. "He's just fine."

Mr. Manning nodded at Mark. "Son, tomorrow I want you to head over to the Johnson ranch and help him fix any fences that might cause more problems for him."

"Yes, sir." Mark nodded.

Claire's brows rose. "Wow, that's really nice of you. Do you always help him out?"

"Out here, we help each other out. Mr. Johnson is getting older and he doesn't have five grown sons still living on his ranch to help out." Mr. Manning smiled at Claire, then looked to each of his sons, who all returned his smile.

"Is it normal for grown sons to live on their family ranch?" Claire had wondered why all of them still lived there. But since they were all single, she had not really thought much about it.

"It is when it's a family-run ranch and not a corporate one." Mr. Manning took a drink of his sweet tea and set it back in front of him.

"Then what about Mr. Johnson's sons? Did he have any?" Claire asked.

The jovial looks and smiles all disappeared.

Mr. Manning pursed his lips. "He has two full-grown sons who both moved away."

"Why?" Claire hoped she wasn't prying too much, but she truly wanted to understand the ranch life. If the Mannings all still lived at home and worked their ranch, were they normal? Or were they the exception?

Matthew sighed. "Steve Johnson married a woman who took over her family ranch, so he moved to South Dakota when he married."

Mrs. Manning took up the conversation as she began putting dishes on the table. "Cal Johnson moved away when he turned eighteen and we haven't seen him since." She looked at her husband, who winced.

There was a story here, Claire knew it, but she would not pry. Instead, she got up from her chair, hoping to change the mood. It had become quite heavy, and it appeared that everyone, including Harper, did not want to talk about Cal. "Here, let me help you, Mrs. Manning." She walked over to the stove and picked up a covered dish and brought it over to the table.

"Thank you, dear. That's very sweet." Mrs. Manning put a hand on Claire's shoulder and gave it a light squeeze. She was grateful for the help, but more than that, she was glad Claire was not asking any more questions.

Harper looked around the table. "Where's Luke and Callie?"

A chuckle escaped Matthew before he could catch it. "Luke decided his girlfriend needed a night on the town." He waggled his brows.

Mark laughed. "I think he's dyin' to propose, but the last

time he asked, Callie made it clear that she wanted to wait a little while longer."

"Really? Do you think she'll say yes this time?" Harper's eyes were wide, and she could not sit still.

Harper loved Callie and thought she and Luke made a perfect couple. She hoped the two would hurry up and get married. But for some strange reason that no one quite understood, she wanted to wait at least a year before they even got engaged.

Claire had not met Luke or Callie yet. But Matthew assured her she would meet them both soon. Luke still lived at home, but he had left before she arrived. And while she napped, it seemed he had come home and then left again. She could not wait to meet the couple.

The Manning brothers all looked at each other and shrugged.

"Who knows what a woman will say." Mark began to put food on his plate, but waited to eat anything until his pops said grace.

Mrs. Manning slapped Mark's hand. "Manners, Mark. You know the rules. The guests get served first." She looked to Claire and Harper. "Please, serve yourselves first. If you don't, there may not be anything left once the boys get ahold of the plates."

Harper laughed. "Ain't that the truth." She put a slice of roast beef on her plate and passed the dish to Claire, who sat to her left.

Once everyone had finished eating and the dishes were cleared away, Harper asked Claire to take her to her room so she could examine her patient.

"Well, what do you think?" Harper asked as she took out her stethoscope from her bag and set it on the bed next to Claire.

Claire furrowed her brows and frowned. "About what?"

Harper stood up and put her hands on her hips. "About the Mannings, of course." She tsk'd and went back to unloading her equipment.

Claire thought about it for a minute before responding. "Well, I haven't spent much time with them yet. But they all seem very nice. I think I'm going to like it here. I can't wait to see the ranch tomorrow. Matthew promised to show me around." All Claire wanted to do was see the horses.

"Just remember, no riding for at least three days. We don't need to see you back in the clinic because you fell off or had a dizzy spell." The nurse put her stethoscope on, took the blood pressure cuff off the bed, and began to work on her patient.

Once Nurse Harper was done, she smiled at Claire. "Looks like the country air is already doing you well. Other than right before dinner, have you experienced any more headaches?"

Her hand went to her temples, and she rubbed at them. "Yeah, I've had a few. But it's mostly been when I've tried to force a memory."

Harper pursed her lips. "And now?"

Claire blinked and pulled her hand away from her head. "Oh, it's a minor ache. I don't even think I need ibuprofen for it."

"Were you trying to remember something?" Harper took out her notes and began to write down what she had observed.

"No. It's just been a minor ache off and on all through dinner. It's basically gone now." Claire smiled and tried to hide the minor pain she still felt. She hated taking pills and briefly wondered if that was normal for her, or a new thing.

The nurse dug in her bag and pulled out a pill pack.

"Here, take these now. I don't want you to lose out on any sleep tonight. It's very important you get plenty of rest while you recover." Harper handed her a pack of two Advil Liqui-Gels.

Claire went to her bedside table, picked up the glass of water sitting there, and took the pills. "How long do you think it will be before it no longer hurts when I try to remember anything?" She was not mad as much as she was frustrated. She knew her memories were there, just waiting for her to grab them. Not being able to do so was starting to get to her.

Harper sighed, and her shoulders slumped. "I really couldn't say. It's possible you'll wake up tomorrow morning with all your memories intact. But highly unlikely. Most likely it'll be a few weeks. In some cases it's taken longer."

"So basically, you've got no clue." Claire pursed her lips and shook her head. She gritted her teeth in expectation of a headache from the movement of her head, and when nothing hurt, she smiled. "I s'pose I'll just have to wait and see how it goes?"

"I'm sorry, but that's all we can say at this point. Just remember to not force it. The brain's a tricky organ. Be sure to get plenty of rest and eat right. When you come back in to see the doctor later this week, he should have more to tell you."

"Well, I guess eating right isn't going to be a problem. Not if that supper was any indication of what it's like around here." Claire smiled.

Harper chuckled. "Why do you think the doctor volunteered me to come out every day?"

"I take it you don't really need to see me daily?" Claire asked, not sure if it was a good or a bad thing.

Harper shook her head. "Probably every other day would

be fine this first week, but I'll never turn down a meal with the Mannings." Her face lit up when she thought about all the barbecue she'd consumed over the years at the Mannings' Triple J Ranch. "One thing you should know is that no one turns down a supper invitation to the Triple J. And they almost always have guests. It's a pretty popular place."

"Yeah, I can see why."

"Alright, so back to your care. Be sure you take the ibuprofen for the next few days. It'll help with the aches and pains as well as the headaches. And everyone here has my cell number." Harper stopped and gave Claire a quizzical look. "Do you have a cell phone? I don't remember there being anything on your person at all when you came in. Did Matthew by chance have it?"

She was not sure, but Claire didn't think she had anything at all, not even a purse or wallet on her. "I don't think so. Wouldn't he have used it to call my family?"

Harper nodded. "Yes, but I thought I'd ask just in case. Alright. I'll get you a cell phone tomorrow and plug my number as well as the doctor's service number in it in case you have any questions at all."

Claire may not have any memories of who she was, but she did know that cell phones were not cheap, and she had no money. "I'm sorry, but I won't be able to pay you back. At least not until I find out who I am." She bit the inside of her cheek and worried how she would pull her weight around here. Something inside her recoiled at the thought of everyone taking care of her and not being able to pay for her care.

With a hand on Claire's shoulder, Harper smiled warmly at her patient. "Don't worry about it. We have an emergency stash of phones and clothes. If there isn't enough here for you, let me know and I'll bring more in. As for the phone, we keep a few of them on hand for situations like this."

"You mean I'm not the first amnesia case you've taken care of?" Claire could not believe that she was a normal patient in a town as small as Beacon Creek.

"No." Harper laughed. "We here take care of a lot of women in need, so we have a stash of refurbished cell phones that just need activating. And we have an agreement with a local cell phone store to provide access for a few months for free when we activate these phones."

Claire furrowed her brows. "But this is a small town. How could you have enough women in need around here?" She did not like where her mind was taking her, and hoped that abusive husbands were not a common occurrence in this town or its surrounding ranches.

For a moment Harper did not understand what Claire was asking, then it dawned on her and her eyes opened wide. She held up her hands. "No, no. We don't have an issue with spousal abuse here. I'm sure there are fights between husbands and wives at times, but I can't recall anyone coming into the clinic with signs of abuse."

She smiled before continuing, "We have an outreach program for the homeless women in Bozeman. Sadly, there's a large population there run by an awful man. We go to Bozeman at least once a month and hand out essentials as well as take care of any injuries. Once in a while, one of the women will be ready to leave that life and we take her back here and help her to get back on her feet. Sometimes even help the women find their families and reunite."

"Wow, that's really great of you all." Claire rubbed her ear. "Do they stay here, on the Triple J Ranch? Is that why Mrs. Manning had so many clothes for me to choose from?"

Harper nodded. "Yes, the Mannings actually started the

program almost two years ago." She was proud of how she had helped all along the way, and never missed an opportunity to help unless she was on duty at the clinic.

"The Mannings must have hearts of gold to bring homeless women back to their ranch." Claire could not imagine doing that. While she did not know if she was a generous person or not, she could not imagine letting homeless people she did not even know live in her house.

Although, she qualified as homeless for the moment. Her situation might be different from someone who lived on the street, since she had on an expensive wedding dress and high-quality cowboy boots, but she had no clue where she'd lived before she lost her memory. All Claire could do was hope and pray that she was a nice person.

CHAPTER 7

"Mmm." Claire stretched her arms above her head and slowly opened her eyes the next morning. The cottage cheese ceiling above her bed was marked and in need of a good paint job. Actually, she thought they should scrape the ceiling and smooth it out. Maybe even put up some antique molding around the ceiling.

She turned her head toward the window and could have sworn she saw the head of a rooster at the bottom of her window. "Shouldn't that thing be crowing? And not peeping?" She chuckled and sat up slowly in bed before she put her feet on the ground.

Taking her time, she rolled her head and stretched her neck. She had slept very soundly and could not even remember waking up during the night. A few wisps of a dream flitted through her memory, and she decided to let it go instead of trying to force it. Just in case it would give her a headache like trying to recall memories would.

Claire had zero desire for headaches today.

She stared outside the window and saw the rooster strutting away with his head bobbing and the red comb waving with his movement. He was probably heading toward the chicken coop. She smiled, and she realized this all felt normal. When she realized how far up the sun was, she looked at the clock on the other nightstand and stood quickly.

Claire had not realized she had slept so long; it was already after nine in the morning. No wonder the rooster was checking her room. She should have been up and out hours ago. She stopped with her hand on the doorknob and thought about it. There was not a memory telling her she was late, just an innate feeling that she should have already been up and going. Almost twelve hours of sleep could not be normal for her, could it?

She shook her head and opened the door. No one was in the hallway, and all was quiet. Everyone was probably already out and working on the ranch while she slept the day away. Claire headed straight to the kitchen for coffee and breakfast.

No one was in the room, and the table was clear. She went over to the counter and discovered a half pot of hot coffee. She picked up the coffee mug next to the pot and poured herself a cup. Once she had it fixed the way she liked it—lots of creamer and a little sugar—she went over to the kitchen table and sat down.

"Ahhh," she said as she inhaled the sharp aroma of the beans mixed with the vanilla creamer. When she took a sip of the nectar, she immediately relaxed. The way her body reacted to coffee must mean that she was an avid coffee connoisseur. Her body instinctively took to it like a duck to water.

The minor headache that had been developing as she got her coffee prepared and sat at the table began to ebb, and she smiled. Claire sat with her back to the door and looked out the window over the sink. It was a large, two-pane window with yellow gingham curtains tied to the sides so she could look outside at the area behind the house and between the barn.

The barn doors were open, but she did not see anyone working. Two dogs were running around and barking at the horses in the paddock to the side of the barn.

Behind her, unbeknownst to her, were two Mannings.

Mrs. Manning was about to walk into the kitchen and make breakfast for Claire, but her oldest son put a hand on her shoulder and motioned with his head to walk to the living room.

When Matthew was inside the living room and certain that no one else was around to overhear their conversation, he motioned for his ma to take a seat.

"What can I do for you, Matthew?" Mrs. Manning's cheery voice was soft as she too ensured no one could overhear them. In a family as large as theirs, it was not often two people could have a private conversation in one of the family rooms.

Matthew plunked down on the recliner closest to his ma, then sighed. "Is she gonna be alright? The poor girl slept for close to twelve hours." He ran a hand through his hair. "Should I call Harper?"

Judith Manning shook her head and smiled. "Son, she's going to be just fine. All that sleep was exactly what she needed. Her body needs to rest in order to heal itself."

His shoulders relaxed, and he slumped against the back of the easy chair. "That's good. I prayed for her last night and this mornin'. Do you think she's got her memory back yet?"

Judith thought about it for a moment and sighed. "I doubt it, but we won't know until we ask her. What do you say we continue this conversation with the young woman?" She raised her eyebrows. She was not much of a gossip; she left that to the Diner Divas.

When she stood and headed toward the kitchen, her son followed suit.

"Of course. Do you think she'll want to go for a tour of the ranch after breakfast?" He noticed she had nice boots and thought she might feel familiar around a ranch. Maybe seeing what they did on the Triple J would trigger some memories.

"Let's ask her," she said as she entered the kitchen.

The noise behind her startled Claire out of her reverie. It was not that she was thinking about her past. Instead, she was focused on the beauty outside the window in front of her. The dogs had stopped barking and were sniffling around the fence while one of the horses threw its head back as though it was laughing. Something about the scene calmed her spirit, and she continued to sip her hot coffee and wonder if this was a normal morning for her.

She hoped it was.

"Good morning, Claire. How'd you sleep?" Mrs. Manning asked as she walked around the table to get a fresh cup of coffee.

"Oh, good morning, Mrs. Manning. I think I slept a bit too well." Claire chuckled nervously and took another sip of her drink.

"That's good to hear," Matthew replied when he walked in and took the chair next to her.

"Please, call me Judith. No need to be so formal around here." Judith smiled and sat down with a black cup of coffee.

"What, no fresh cup for me?" Matthew teased his mother as he stood to get his own cup.

"Sweetie, why don't you start another pot after you get your cup? I think we'll need it shortly." Judith turned her attention back to Claire. "What would you like for breakfast?"

Claire held a hand up. "Oh, I don't want to be any trouble. Looks like I overslept and missed breakfast. Whatever you have that's quick and easy will be fine."

Judith reached across the table and covered her guest's hand with hers. "Don't go worry'n about that. I love to cook. Do you like omelets?" She squeezed Claire's hand lightly before letting go and standing up to get started on breakfast.

"I'm not sure." Claire's stomach grumbled, and she felt her cheeks heat. She put a hand to her belly and apologized.

"Hmm, sounds like your stomach wants an omelet. How about a Denver omelet?" Mrs. Manning opened the fridge and pulled out the ingredients.

"Um, sure?" Claire shrugged. She was not sure what she liked. The only thing she knew was that she was hungry and it sounded good.

Matthew laughed. "I guess that answers my question."

Claire's brow furrowed. "I'm sorry, did I miss your question?"

He chuckled. "No, I was about to ask if you had any memories back. But if you don't even know what you like for breakfast, then I doubt anythin's come back yet."

"No memories." Claire took another sip of her coffee and thought about how to word her thoughts so far this morning. "Something feels...normal? Well, maybe not normal, but familiar?" She twisted her lips as she thought about it. "I guess I feel like being on a ranch is something I did back home."

Matthew looked at her and asked, "How so? If you don't have any memories, how do you know this feels normal?"

Claire twisted her lips and looked out the window. "I think I must have a kitchen window like yours." She used her coffee mug to point to the window and beyond. "Since I sat down, I've felt like this is a normal morning for me."

"So, you normally sleep the mornin' away before getting a cup of coffee?" he teased.

She laughed. "No, I don't think I normally sleep in." She looked down sheepishly at her cup. "Sorry about that. When I saw the time, I felt like I was really far behind. But when I sat down with my coffee and looked out the back..." She shrugged. "I don't know, I felt comfortable. Like I've done this before." She shook her head. "Sorry, I doubt I'm making any sense."

Judith looked over her shoulder as she mixed the bell pepper into the bowl with eggs, milk, and chopped ham. "Actually, it does make sense. When you went through the box of clothes, you chose comfortable attire that will work on a ranch instead of the pretty sundresses. And your boots, while they might be fashionable, look to be well-worn."

Claire looked down at her feet and smiled. "I know these boots must be my favorite, but I don't know why. They're very comfortable and formed to my feet."

Matthew scooted back in his chair and looked down at the ground. "But they're blue. No cowgirl worth a lick of salt would work in boots like that." He pointed at Claire's feet.

"*Au contraire*—they're turquoise." Claire pointed to her footwear.

Mrs. Manning turned back to her bowl and hid her smile. "Oh, I don't know. She may not muck out a stall in those boots, but she could certainly ride in them, or keep house and cook in them. She could do all sorts of chores that wouldn't get her too dirty."

Claire smirked at Matthew. "See, I just might be a cowgirl worth a lick of salt." She took another sip of her coffee and used her mug to hide her smile.

Matthew snorted. "Right. I know better than to argue with two women about fashion." He narrowed his eyes at their guest. "How about I give you a tour after breakfast? I need to take care of a few emails and place a feed order to pick up later, then I'll come back here and get you for a short tour."

Judith turned around with the bowl in her hands. "No horse riding. You can only tour as far as Claire can comfortably walk." She lifted a brow and stared at her son. "I don't want you to overtax her on her first day here."

"Yes, ma'am." He gave a cowboy salute and stood up. "I'll be back in 'bout half an hour to get you for the nickel tour." Matthew winked at Claire before he headed to the office.

When he finished with his work, he checked his watch. It went faster than he'd expected. Since his friend and brother-in-law Logan came home almost two years ago, the ordering system for the feed store had been updated and it was much quicker and easier to place orders. Logan had also implemented delivery services, but Matthew still preferred to go into town and pick up his orders. It was pretty much the only time he went to town outside of church lately.

Claire took her plate and coffee mug to the sink and began to rinse them when Judith came back into the room. "Oh honey, I can do that. You should get your sweater and get ready for the tour."

"Please, let me help. It's the least I can do since you're taking such great care of me." Claire did not like the idea of Judith cooking and cleaning for her. The woman was such a sweet person, she hated to take advantage her kindness. Plus, she knew she needed to carry her weight here.

"How 'bout you help with supper? Right now you need to get that tour. Just"—she wagged a finger at the young lady—"be sure to no overdo it. I don't need Harper coming out tonight and finding you too exhausted to even eat supper with us, ya hear?"

Claire could not help but smile at the motherly figure in front of her. "Yes, ma'am." She turned and headed for her room, where she brushed her teeth and grabbed the sweater. Even though it was spring and the sun was shining, she could feel the chilly air coming in from the open kitchen window and knew she'd want the warmth.

By the time she was ready and back out in the kitchen, Matthew was there with two travel mugs of coffee in his hands. "Don't worry, I remembered how you liked it—light brown, almost white." He handed her a mug, and she took a sip.

"Mmm. That's really good." She eyed him. "Have you ever worked as a barista?"

Matthew looked at his mother's smirk and returned it. "You could say that."

Claire was not sure what he meant, but she was happy to have someone make her a great cup of coffee and was not about to look a gift horse in the mouth.

CHAPTER 8

Matthew led Claire out the back door and into the paddock area where she had been watching the dogs and horses earlier. "Now, be sure to let me know if you get tired. We won't be goin' far, and there's always somewhere ta sit and take a breather, if you need it."

"Are you worried about your ma getting mad at you?" she asked.

"You bet. Have you met my ma?" He shivered.

Claire chuckled. "Yes, I have. And I can assure you I have no plans to overdo it. I don't need Judith getting on my case, either."

"Smart woman." Luke Manning walked around the open fence gate and smiled. "Hi, I'm Luke. Nice to finally meet ya."

Claire reached out to shake his hand. "Nice to meet you as well. Sorry I wasn't up earlier with the rest of the family."

Luke held up a hand. "Don't worry. I get it. After I was shot last year, I needed a few days of sleep, too. Take as many lazy days as you can get before anyone puts ya ta work."

Claire's eyebrows hit her hairline. "Shot?" She was not

sure what she had gotten herself into. Could these folks be into illegal activities? If so, she was not the least bit interested in staying there. She took a couple steps back.

Luke help up his hands. "Oh, no. No. I was helpin' the local sheriff stop cattle rustlers and got in front of a shotgun."

Claire swallowed hard and took a deep breath. "Are you a deputy?"

"No. Well...not exactly."

"His fiancé is a deputy," Matthew interjected, and slapped his brother on his back.

Luke pursed his lips and glared at his big brother. "Not yet."

"Really? She said no again?" Matthew took his cowboy hat off and ran a rugged hand through his messy hair.

Luke shook his head. "I didn't ask. I was gonna, but as I began to bring up the subject, she must have known what I was gonna do and she told me she still wasn't ready."

Matthew shook his head. "Sorry, man. I know she loves you. But that ex of hers must have done a real number on her."

"No, I think it's that once she says yes, she's gonna be in weddin' mode. With her new job, she just doesn't have the time to focus on anythin' but getting' her testin' out of the way. It won't be much longer." Luke had been planning on proposing the day Callie passed her last deputy exam, but he couldn't wait and wanted to get his ring on her right away. Normally he was a patient man, but with Callie he could not wait.

"Wait." Claire put up her hand. "Your girlfriend's a sheriff's deputy and you helped her stop rustlers and got shot? Are you serious?" She looked around. "Is it dangerous here?"

Matthew walked closer to Claire and took her hand.

"Don't worry, Claire. We stopped the gang of rustlers. They're all in jail."

"Yup. And the sheriff said it was very rare for us to have to deal with somethin' like that here in these parts." Luke nodded. "It's very safe here, you've nothin' t' worry 'bout."

Claire's shoulders visibly relaxed, and she released a breath she did not realize she'd been holding. "That's good to know." She looked at Luke. "Where were you shot?"

Luke chuckled and lifted his right arm. "Good as new. It was through and through and didn't do much damage, thankfully."

His brother slapped his right shoulder and chuckled. "Yup, and now he's got a right nice scar to show off to the guys." Matthew turned to look at Claire. "And let me tell ya, he shows it off ev'ry chance he gets."

"Hey!" Luke slapped his brother's back and turned to their guest. "Don't listen t' my brother. Next thing ya know, he'll be telling you tall tales of our childhood." Luke chuckled and shook his head. He loved his brother, but sometimes Matthew just did not know when to keep his pie hole shut.

Claire laughed at the antics of the two cowboys in front of her. "I sure hope I have a brother or sister who I joke around with like you two do."

Matthew and Luke sobered up quickly, and it was all Matthew could do to keep from reaching out to comfort the lost little filly. "I'm sorry…"

Claire held up a hand. "Nope. Don't." She shook her head. "I love that you guys wrestle and joke around. It actually made me forget my troubles for a few minutes." She paused, and then a slow smile spread across her face. "No pun intended."

Her joke seemed to lighten the heavy mood that had begun to develop, and both cowboys laughed.

"Alright, I gotta go check the fence lines in the back forty." Luke looked up at the developing clouds. "I'll see ya all later for supper. Callie's coming over after her shift, so you'll get ta meet her tonight." He waved and smiled at his brother and the pretty lady next to him before strutting off to get his horse.

Claire watched Luke walk away with that cowboy swagger and smiled. "I like your brother. He's a hoot."

"You say that now, but wait until you get to know him better. Or better yet, wait until you see him at supper tonight. Just watch your biscuit. He's been known to steal a few from unsuspecting guests." Matthew winked at his partner and motioned for her to come closer to the horse who had hung her head over the fence.

Claire walked up to the mare and held her hand out for the horse to smell her. "Oh, you're a pretty one, aren't you?" She looked at the black mare with gray patches and began to stroke her forehead.

"Huh." Matthew hooked his thumbs in his belt loops. "Looks like you're either a natural, or you know horses." He walked up next to her and ran a hand down the horse's mane. "Whiskers here loves attention."

"Is she your horse?" Claire didn't take her eyes off Whiskers, or she would have seen the way Matthew's head jerked back.

"Mine? You think I ride a small mare?" He was not sure if he was offended or shocked. Maybe a little of both. Whiskers was one of their shorter horses at only fifteen and a half hands. She was also one of their calmest ones. Not really his speed.

Chloe, Matthew's sister, used to ride Whiskers. Nowadays it was Callie who rode her.

"Okay, Mr. Macho. If you don't ride this gorgeous horse, then which one do you ride?" She put her hands on her hips and raised a brow.

He grabbed her hand. "Alright, come with me and I'll show you my stallion." He smirked and pulled her inside the barn where his horse, Thunder, waited impatiently for his treat.

Claire followed Matthew inside and noticed the stalls full of other horses. It made sense they would have a lot since there were so many of them in the family, but if she counted right, there were more than enough for each family member —including Elizabeth and her husband, who did not live on the ranch—to each have two horses. "Why so many horses?"

"We also breed horses. Several of the stallions here are studs that no longer get ridin' on a regular basis. Then we have a few mares, and there are a few new members of the family waitin' to be sold when they're weaned from their mommas." Matthew rubbed the forehead of one such momma as she stuck her head over the top of the gate. Probably hoping to get a treat.

"Oh, she's so cute!" Claire practically squealed when she saw a little filly hiding behind her momma a few stalls down. She squatted and smiled at the horse, making cooing sounds like it was a human baby.

The little horse's whinny sounded almost like Claire's squeal. He might have to name her Squeakers if they kept her.

"What's her name?" Claire's face lit up like the sky on the Fourth of July during the fireworks display.

Something inside him stuttered and pounded against his chest. He almost rubbed at the ache in his chest, but decided he needed to ignore it. She was a newly married woman. And totally off-limits. Of course, his heart *would* beat for a woman he could not have.

Matthew shook his head and smirked. "Squeakers, if we keep her."

She pursed her lips. "Get real. That's not an appropriate name for such a beautiful horse." She looked back at the all-black foal. "I think you should call her Beauty."

He snorted. "Now who's coming up with silly names? Do you know how many black horses are called Beauty?" It was a good name, but no way would he do something so common.

She stood up. "Well, give her a silly name if you want, but I still think Beauty suits her. It'll give her something great to live up to. Especially if you read her the book at night."

"Read a book to a horse? Are you serious?" He bellowed out a laugh and almost had to bend over. He had never heard something so silly.

"Why not?" Claire shrugged and looked at the momma. She ran her hand along the mare's neck and cooed at her, too. "You'd like to have your little filly read to, wouldn't you? Maybe I'll come back here after supper and read to y'all."

"Oh boy." He shook his head. "Come on, Thunder's down here."

She eyed him. "Thunder? Talk about a typical name."

"Wait until you see him." He chuckled and made his way to the back of the barn, where he kept his large steed.

"Huh, well." She put a finger to her lower lip and tapped it while she took in the large, silver-white horse that was eyeing her up and down. He seemed to be taking her in, just like she was him. "I guess the name does make sense."

Matthew's horse was almost seventeen hands high with a stark white patch that went down the slope of the horse's head like a lightning bolt.

"I guess it's better than Lightning." She grinned and put

her hand out for the horse to sniff. With her palm flat and under his muzzle, he sniffled her hand and lifted his head. When the horse looked her in the eyes, she smiled in return. "You really are a handsome one, aren't you?"

The horse whinnied and nodded his head. He seemed to have understood what she said and agreed with her.

"Well, I do think you might be a bit too much like your rider." Claire winked at the horse, who blinked in response, and she laughed.

"Here, give him a carrot and he'll love ya forever." Matthew handed her the orange treat with the green stalk still attached and stood back, watching the little filly interact with his American Quarter Horse. "Actually, I think he might already love you."

She held the carrot in her hand behind her back as she ran a hand down Thunder's mane. When she looked back over her shoulder, she grinned and winked.

Matthew had to take a deep breath and two more steps back from the alluring cowgirl in front of him. If he weren't careful, he'd fall hard for her and get his heart broken.

CHAPTER 9

C laire missed lunch, which was a blessing if Matthew was being honest with himself. He had been *off* ever since their tour. Even now, in his truck on his way to town, he could not get her out of his mind. He was not sure how he was going to act next time he saw her.

The woman was married, and an amnesiac. But all he could think of was her scent and her laugh. Every time he got close to her, he picked up hints of lavender, cut grass, and something sweet that must have been all her. His senses kicked into overdrive and he constantly had to remind himself she was married. No matter how much he did not want her to be, she was off-limits.

Maybe spending some time in town with his buddies would help him get his mind in gear.

He could not believe a half hour had already passed when he pulled up to the feed store. Matthew must have thought about the pretty filly his entire trip to town. He would have to listen to a sermon for his trip home. Maybe if he prayed and focused more on God, he would be able to get his mind to behave.

"Who am I kidding?" he mumbled as he stepped out of his truck.

The bell above the door to the feed store rang when he opened it. No one paid him mind; they were all at the front corner watching the latest checkers challenge taking place between the old gents.

Those older cowboys had once run this small town. Now they hung out in the feed store playing games and watching the town amble on by. They also gossiped. Although, not nearly as bad as the Diner Divas, who practically owned seats at the counter over at Rosie's Diner.

If anyone missed out on gossip, all they had to do was come play checkers with the guys, or head over to the diner and speak with the divas and they'd know more about the residents of their tiny town than anyone ever needed to know.

That thought stopped him in his tracks. Matthew wondered what the town was saying about Claire. He hoped they were being nice. But, maybe…just maybe, someone knew who she was, or at least where she came from. He would have to ask around while he was there.

Matthew walked up to Logan and shook his brother-in-law's hand. "So, who's winning this time, and what's their bet?"

The old men who played checkers here every day would do monthly tournaments to keep things from getting stale. They never bet money—it was usually something to do with barbecue.

"Well, it seems the guys have decided to sweeten the pot this time." Logan chuckled.

"Really? Did they up the ante to money?" Matthew did not think they would, but one never knew with these old coots.

Logan shook his head. "Nah, nothing so simple. Loser has to ask his girl to marry 'em."

If Matthew had been drinking something, he would have spit it out. Never had he heard something so absurd. "But... but, they don't all have girlfriends, do they?"

"Nope. Only Charlie Macon has a girl right now. I think the others are tired of Charlie not commitin' to Ms. Barton. Everyone thinks the two should just get on with it. You know?" Logan chuckled and shook his head.

"So, it's a conspiracy to get Mr. Macon to marry the old school teacher? I think I like this one." He rubbed his hands together and licked his lips. While Matthew tried to stay out of the town gossip, he had wondered why the two had not tied the knot yet. Anyone looking at them could tell they were both in love.

"I prefer it when they play for barbecue. At least then I usually get some of the winnings." Logan shook his head. What he really wanted was a family barbecue out at the Triple J. With their latest guest, he figured they would be calling him any time to invite him and Elizabeth over for a Saturday supper.

The two walked away, and Logan helped Matthew load up his order. Before Logan could get back into the store, Matthew called out, "Hey, why don't you and Elizabeth come to supper on Saturday? I think we'll be barbecuin' steaks." He smiled, knowing his brother-in-law would never turn down Triple J barbecued steak.

Logan grinned and nodded his head. "I hoped that'd be the case. Say, how's your newest guest? Has she remembered anything yet?"

He shook his head. "Nope. Not yet. But the doctor did say it could be several weeks or longer." Matthew shrugged, not really sure if he wanted Claire to get her memory back soon or stay with them longer.

He should want her to get her memory back so she could find her family and get home, and out of his life. But he was a selfish man. If she never got her memory back, did that mean she was still married?

He really did need more sermons and time in the Bible with God. Even if she did not know who she was, she was still married. Matthew waved as Logan turned to head back into the store and he got in his truck and headed to Rosie's Diner. Matthew was even more determined to find out who that girl was, and who she was married to.

Maybe he should even stop in to see if the sheriff had any more news before heading home.

Once Matthew had parked his truck, he headed into the diner, not really sure how to ask the town's gossipers about Claire. If he outright asked them, they would think he was interested in the wrong way. The last thing he and Claire needed was to have the town gossiping about an affair between them.

He would never act on his feelings, so there was nothing to worry about.

In fact, the more he thought about it, the more he realized it was just a temporary bout of insanity. It was probably just because he rescued her. Had he met her on the street here in town, he doubted he would even notice her.

Well, he might notice her. She was a bit too pretty to not notice. But his heart would not beat like a drum when she was near.

With his hand on the handle, he took a deep breath and prepared to enter the lion's den.

There was so much chatter in the diner, he was not sure if

he'd be able to overhear anything about Claire even if they were talking about her.

The first thing Matthew noticed when he stepped inside, besides the smell of bacon grease, was the pink pouf of Cindy Macon, Charlie Macon's sister-in-law. She had worn her hair the same way as far back as Matthew could remember. It always reminded him of the pink cotton candy they sold at the carnivals the town hosted several times a year.

He stepped up to the counter and ordered a bacon cheese-burger, fries, and a Coke. He would be late for lunch, so he might as well eat there before heading home. It was rare he was in town for lunch, and if he ate there, he might have a chance of discovering something about Claire.

Hopefully, something useful.

"I heard she left her husband at the altar and hitchhiked with a trucker! When he got a little too friendly, she jumped out and that's how she hurt herself." Lou Ann Dobbs crossed her boney arms over her chest and nodded her head while she pursed her lips.

While he did not want Claire to have had a bad run-in with a trucker, he did hope she ran from her fiancé before saying their *I do's*. Guilt flooded his system the second he thought it, and he chastised himself for wanting something so awful. No, he would have to pray for the Lord to take these feelings away from him. And not spend so much time with her.

Martha Stanhope shook her head, and the long gray pony-tail swished along her back. "Nuh-uh, I heard they were in a car accident twenty miles away and she left her husband in the car to go get help. The poor thing has no clue how she got this far away."

Lou Ann Dobbs clucked her tongue, and the extra skin on her

neck jiggled when she shook her head. "No, dear. The poor girl has amnesia. I heard from Becky, who heard from Carol, who heard from the neighbor of Doc Montgomery, that she was found on the side of the road and brought to town in her wedding dress. They don't know where her groom is, but she's married." The elderly woman's head bobbed up and down in dramatic moves, as though she was the only one who knew the absolute truth.

The woman turned her head to Matthew, who had just finished placing his order. "Matthew, dear, aren't you the one who found her? Surely you know more about her, right?"

He held his hands up and leaned back. "Whoa, I don't know any more than you do. I did find her, and her name's Claire. But that's all I know."

Mary Walters smiled like she knew a secret, and Matthew felt like he was in for some trouble when the woman opened her mouth.

"I heard she's staying with you and your family at the Triple J. How is it you don't know anything more?" The older woman nodded and smirked.

"What? No one told me that's where she got to." Lou Ann turned back to Matthew. "Why didn't you say something, Matthew? You know this is the biggest story in town since your family stopped the cattle rustlers." She leaned her elbows on the counter and stared the oldest Manning son down.

With all four divas staring him down, Matthew felt his throat tighten. Maybe he had made a mistake coming here to get information. He should have remembered how these women always weaseled stories out of everyone they set their sights on.

He knew he was in trouble when the ringleader, Cindy Macon, stood up and sauntered over to stand over his shoulder. She leaned down and whispered, "How about you share with us? We only want to help get the word out so her family can find her."

Matthew knew she did not want to help—she just wanted more juicy gossip to spread. He cleared his dry throat. "Honest, ladies, I don't know any more than you do at this point."

"Alright, leave the poor cowboy alone." Rosie stood in front of him at the counter and made a shooing motion toward Cindy. "If you don't play nice, I'll have to ban you, again." She raised her brows at all four divas and put her hands on her hips.

"Oh, you know you love having us in here." Mary Walters tried to sweet-talk the stern-looking diner owner, but she was not having any of it.

"Ladies, how many times must I warn you about what the Good Book says regarding gossip?" She eyed each Diner Diva slowly before continuing. "Do I need to get the pastor to come over and remind you?"

All four women sat back in their bar stools and looked a bit sheepish.

"I'm sorry. I do know better. It's just…" Martha Stanhope looked around and frowned. "There's just not much to do around here right now."

"Uh-huh. How about you head out to the churches and see who needs some help? I bet if you really wanted something to keep you busy, you'd find a whole passel of good deeds to do." Rosie clucked her tongue and looked back at Matthew. "Sorry, sweetie, sometimes I just don't know what to do with them ladies."

Matthew had never seen anyone put the Diner Divas in their place. And from the sounds of it, Rosie did it often. "No problem. And I know Pastor Baker could use some help this week. He's assistin' Elizabeth with puttin' together care packs for the homeless."

Rosie clapped her hands. "Perfect!" She turned her head to the Diner Divas. "Ladies, did you hear Matthew? Once you're done with your lunch, why don't you head on over to the Beacon Creek Baptist Church and do some good this afternoon?" It was more of an order than a request.

The ladies all sat up straight and smiled.

"Why I do say, that sounds like a plan." Cindy smiled and looked between her friends. "I've been wantin' to get involved with this here initiative. What do you say, girls? You up for the challenge?"

The other ladies tittered amongst themselves, and Matthew relaxed. Elizabeth had told him that those ladies just needed a project and they would stop gossiping so much, but he didn't realize how on the mark she was.

By the time his meal came the Diner Divas had left, and he relaxed into his lunch with a smile.

"Sorry about them. They really do have good hearts." Rosie sighed and wiped down the counter space next to his.

"Do they have anything to do besides spend time at the beauty parlor and hang out here?" Matthew had not seen them anywhere else, except church when they had services. But didn't some of them have grandchildren they could visit?

"Not really. Pastor asked me just the other day if I thought they might help to organize a few events at the churches this spring. That's partly why I sent them to the Baptist church. With their annual fundraiser coming up, Pastor has to need some help."

Matthew took a bite of his juicy burger and nodded. He knew the Methodist and Catholic churches also had fundraisers coming up. Spring was usually a busy time in town as well as out on the ranches and farms. None of the Diner Divas had jobs, and with nothing else to do, he guessed gossiping would be an easy way to pass the time until all the events started up.

Well, Matthew did not learn anything new about Claire, but he did learn something about the divas. He would have to ask Elizabeth on Saturday if she could help keep those ladies busy.

CHAPTER 10

After the tour, Claire was exhausted. She didn't want to tell Matthew that she was tired. Instead, she kept going and looking at all the horses and talking to them as though they were already her friends. And in her heart, she knew they were.

After greeting Judith, she told her she needed a nap before lunch. They'd only been out for just under two hours, but all the walking and bantering back and forth with Matthew had worn her out.

Harper had warned her that she'd be tired for a few days. While she didn't lose a lot of blood, she was dehydrated and had lost enough blood that her body would need rest, food, and plenty of water to replenish everything she'd lost. Not to mention the healing needed in her brain. Claire just wasn't prepared to feel so exhausted after only a little while outside.

She had the feeling that she was a very active sort, and loved animals. Horses seemed to be the animal of her heart. Maybe she was a veterinarian like Elizabeth? Or could she be a rancher like Matthew? She fell asleep wondering what her life had been like before her accident.

When she awoke, it was to a nightmare. She felt herself rolling around in her blanket and sat up straight with a scream. After she took a few deep breaths, her heart calmed down and she looked around.

The door to her room slammed open. "What's wrong?" Matthew looked around wide-eyed, expecting to find a stranger in her room, or something.

Claire's hand went to her heart and it started beating erratically again. "Nothing. Sorry, I think I had a bad dream." The ghostly wisps of two indistinct faces left her feeling cold and wondering what she'd dreamt of.

His shoulders relaxed, and he took in a deep breath. Behind him were his mother and father.

"Are you alright? What happened?" Mr. Manning asked as he looked around her room and noted the window was closed and latched.

Claire's cheeks burned, and she felt terrible. "I'm sorry. I didn't realize I was so loud. Did the entire house hear me?" She couldn't bring herself to look the Mannings in their faces. Embarrassment flooded her system, and she wished she could hide under her covers and go back in time.

"Oh, sweetie. Don't worry. We were actually just down the hall heading toward the kitchen. I doubt anyone else heard. If they had, they'd be here by now." Judith pushed past her husband and son to enter the room and comfort her guest.

"Thanks, I think?" Claire put her face in her hands and shivered.

Judith sat down on the bed next to Claire. "Do you remember your dream?"

She shook her head. "Not really. It's all just a terrible feeling now. Something bad happened in my dream, but I can't recall it." Claire rubbed her temple where a headache had begun.

"Let me get you some Advil. When was the last time you took any?" Matthew offered.

Without looking up, Claire answered, "At breakfast. What time is it now?"

"It's two. So it's past time you had some medicine." Matthew left the room and headed to the kitchen where they kept a bottle of Advil Liqui-Gels. He took two gel capsules and filled a glass with water before heading back to Claire's room.

Judith rubbed Claire's back and told her she was safe.

They sat there quietly, and Claire turned her head to look out the window. A storm had rolled in and sheets of rain were pouring outside her window. In one sense it was calming, but it also meant she'd be stuck indoors until the rain subsided. She itched to get back outside and spend more time with the horses.

"Here, take these. It'll help." Matthew walked up to her and handed her the medicine and glass of water.

She looked up through her lashes and gave him a half smile. "Thanks." Claire took the pills and downed them with the water. Then she lay back in bed. "I can't believe I've slept so much today. What's wrong with me?"

A hand squeezed her arm lightly, and when she opened her eyes she saw Judith's understanding eyes looking back at her. "I think you should expect to sleep a lot for at least the next week. When Harper comes tonight, we can ask her for more information about how much you need to sleep." Judith stood up. "When you're ready, I saved you a sandwich. We also have homemade macaroni salad and pickles."

"Ma makes the best pickles around. I hope you like dill pickles." Matthew took the empty glass from Claire and held it.

"Thanks, that really does sound great. Give me a few

minutes? I'll be right in." Claire could not believe she'd slept for close to three hours and missed another family meal. She'd have to start setting alarms so she didn't cause any extra work for Judith, or the family.

Judith patted her shoulder. "No worries. I'll go and get it plated for you. Come out when you're ready."

Everyone left the room, and Claire sighed heavily before throwing back the covers and getting out of bed.

When Judith walked to the kitchen, she pulled her son with her. "Matthew, I'm worried about her."

He nodded. "So am I, Ma. If she was havin' a nightmare, it makes me wonder what happened to her before I found her." His nose flared and his hands fisted. Matthew knew that if he ever found the person who had harmed her, he'd…well, he'd hit the man for certain. Then he would haul the sorry excuse for a human right to the sheriff and demand he be imprisoned.

Matthew was not normally a violent man, but anyone who would harm a little filly like Claire, well…he deserved a knuckle sandwich and then some.

Judith shook her head. "I'm not sure what happened to the poor girl, but I think she's going to need friends." She gave her son a knowing look. "No admirers." Her left brow lifted.

The guilty feelings came back, and he shuffled his feet. "Ma, I just want to help her. I know she is married and in a lot of trouble. She needs our help."

"Mm-hm." She turned toward the refrigerator and began to take out all the fixings to make Claire a small lunch. "As long as you remember that, son."

Later that evening after Harper arrived, they all sat down to supper.

The rain had stopped almost as quickly as it had begun. With a mostly clear sky, Claire hoped that the next day would bring cooler weather and a chance to get back out to the horses, and maybe even into town.

"Thanks, Judith, for allowing me to join you every night for supper. This roasted chicken beats microwaved lasagna any day of the week." Harper chuckled before taking another bite of the juicy chicken breast on her plate.

"Harper, dear, you're always welcome here. I hope you know that." Mrs. Manning beamed at Harper. Since Harper was best friends with Judith's daughters from a young age, the nurse had been a regular at their supper table. Especially during the summers when she'd stay the night, or the week, with the twins on the ranch when her parents allowed it.

Judith always loved a full table, and a full house. If she could have had more children, she would have. But the good Lord had given her seven wonderful kids, and she could not complain.

Once Judith brought out dessert, a homemade apple pie with vanilla bean ice cream, Matthew took the chance to ask Harper a few questions about Claire.

"How much should Claire be sleeping? She's worried she's sleeping too much." Matthew took a bite of the warm pie and melting ice cream.

"Well, it just depends on how tired she is." Harper turned to Claire. "How much have you been sleeping?"

Claire put her fork down on her plate and wiped her mouth with a napkin after she finished the bite she already had in her mouth. "Last night, I slept almost eleven hours and then this afternoon I took about a three-hour nap. Doesn't that seem like too much sleep?"

The nurse shook her head. "That sounds about right. I'm sure you'll sleep good tonight as well. Don't worry about sleeping more than normal right now. Your brain needs the downtime to fix any missing connections between memory and consciousness. It's all completely normal. I'd be worried if you weren't sleeping so much."

"See, I told you it was fine." Matthew smirked before taking another bite.

"Alright, I won't worry, for now. But how much longer should it be before I don't sleep so much? While I still don't remember anything, I do get the feeling that I'm not one to laze about all day."

"Getting antsy to get out and about?" Harper asked.

Claire nodded. "Yes, and I so want to ride a horse." She could not help but smile when she thought about Whiskers, Thunder, and all the other horses in the barn she'd met that morning.

"Whoa, now. You know you can't ride yet. And when you do take your first ride, you need to take it slow and easy. No galloping, and especially no racing." Harper raised a brow and looked to Matthew.

He raised his hands. "Whoa, I had no plans to race Claire any time soon."

Harper pointed a finger at him. "But you do have plans. I want you to promise me you'll wait until you see the doctor on Monday before you let her do anything more than a slow, sedate pace. And only on Whiskers."

A slow smile crept across Luke's face. "Whiskers sure is popular lately, isn't she?" He and Callie were with the family for dinner that night but hadn't had much of a chance to talk with Claire yet.

"Oh, no. I couldn't. Isn't Whiskers Callie's horse?" Claire looked to the young woman she had just met and smiled apologetically. She had no desire to steal someone else's horse.

"Well, she's not really *my* horse. She actually belongs to Chloe. I just get to ride her since no one else does." Callie smiled at Claire. "Please, feel free to ride Whiskers as much as you're allowed. I don't get to ride as much as I'd like these days."

Callie was getting close to finishing her deputy classes and needed to study most nights. She had only been getting out to the ranch about three nights a week, and wasn't always able to ride the horse when she did visit.

Judith nodded. "I agree, Whiskers is the best horse for Claire right now." She looked to her eldest son. "And I want to stress how important it is for you to follow Nurse Harper's orders, son."

"What? Are you all gangin' up on me?" Matthew chuckled. He'd never let Claire run rampant on a horse, especially when he didn't even know how much she knew about riding.

Harper laughed. "All I can think of is the summers I spent here growing up and watching you race not only your brothers, but both of your sisters, and anyone else crazy enough to agree to racing."

"Fine, fine. I do love a good race, but not with a little lady still recovering from a brain injury." He looked at Claire. "Sorry, but I'm gonna have to agree with Harper and the doctor. We'll take it easy and go accordin' to their rules."

Claire had the feeling she was a good horsewoman, but since she could not remember, she'd follow the rules and feel it all out. The last thing she needed was to fall and hit her head again. Just the idea of sitting atop a horse made her smile. "Of course. I don't want to get anyone in trouble."

After dinner everyone went outside to the fire pit and sat around the campfire enjoying the last vestiges of the sunset and sipping sweet tea. With the storm having passed, the setting sun had hit the remaining clouds just enough to make them look like balloons and streamers in various shades of reds and oranges.

Claire especially loved the long, fluffy clouds that looked more like beds of hay than anything else. There was something calming and familiar about the sky that night.

They all spent a wonderful evening chatting and joking. Claire took a deep breath and inhaled the fresh, clean air that's only available after a good, strong storm passes through. In that moment, she was content to be right where she was, with the people around her.

But Claire knew that Harper needed to get going home, so they got up and went inside to get her exam over with.

Harper left after examining Claire. While Claire wanted to spend the entire evening outside enjoying the clean air and the great conversations going around, she also felt herself fading just a bit. If she wanted to be up and have breakfast with the family, she knew she'd have to hit the hay soon.

But first, she headed back outside for just a bit more of the fireside chat.

"And do you remember when Luke turned thirteen and got his new horse?" The Mannings had been telling stories mostly about Luke, since his girlfriend Callie was there. But since most of the stories included tales about all the siblings, Claire enjoyed hearing them and didn't want to leave.

"Oh, please tell me he did something funny, like use the wrong saddle?" Callie was eating up all the tales of her boyfriend's childhood and just loving it.

Luke put up his hands. "Alright, I think we've shared enough about me tonight. How about we focus on Matthew?" He looked at his brother and gave a curt shake of his head.

Matthew knew his brother did not want this story told, but it was too juicy not to share it. Besides, Callie needed to know what she was getting into.

A mischievous grin crossed Matthew's face, and the rest of the family began laughing. "Well, I guess if you don't want your girlfriend to know how well you could race and stop on a dime, who am I to tell?"

Callie clapped her hands. "Ohhh, do tell!"

Mark leaned in and grinned. "It was the first day he had Rascal, and he was bound and determined to make sure we all knew he was no longer a kid and knew how ta handle his horse."

The family broke out into laughter again, and red stained Luke's cheeks before he put his hands over his face. "No, no. Please don't."

"Sorry, bro. Your little lady wants the story, and as a gentleman, it's my job to do her biddin'." Mark chuckled and went on to tell the story of how Luke stopped his horse too quickly, and too close to the little river that ran through their land.

"Thankfully, it was early summer and the creek was still flowing nicely." Mark looked at his brother and grinned. "Rascal did stop on a dime, but Luke wasn't prepared for the jolt and he fell over the horse's head and right into the creek!"

Claire could not help but laugh with the rest of the family. Poor Luke. His girlfriend was also laughing. Eventually, Luke joined in and took the razzing graciously from his brothers.

"Well, at least I got up and got back in the saddle." Luke eyed Mark, and a cheese-eating grin spread across his face. "Which reminds me of a time one of my brothers didn't get back in the saddle for several weeks." He arched a brow at Mark, who wiped the smile off his face and slumped in his chair.

As much as Claire wanted to hear these stories and laugh with the family, she knew she needed to get to bed before she fell asleep in her chair.

When she stood up, all eyes flew to her and Luke stopped telling the story of his brother's fall from Glory. His horse was actually named Glory. She was still laughing and shaking her head, but had to make her goodnights and get going.

"Sleep tight. And don't worry about sleepin' in t'morrow. Be sure to let yourself get all the sleep your body needs." Matthew loved being around her, but her rest was more important than having breakfast with the little filly.

She waved and went inside. When she made it to her room, she set her alarm for six-thirty. That should give her enough time to get ready and out to help with a seven o'clock breakfast.

From what she had learned, the boys all went out first thing in the morning and fed the animals before they came in for a hot-cooked meal from their mother.

If she could get out there early enough, maybe she could even help Judith prepare breakfast.

CHAPTER 11

The best-laid plans, and all that.

Claire slept through her alarm and didn't wake until after breakfast, again. But this time it was a little bit earlier than the day before. She'd call that progress, but still hoped to be up in time to enjoy the meal with the family before they all began their day.

When she hurriedly entered the kitchen, Judith was washing dishes and no one else was in the room. "Good morning. I'm sorry I'm late, again." Claire shook her head and sighed.

The coffee pot was empty. However, percolating sounds and the aroma of fresh-brewed beans drifted through her olfactory senses and she relaxed. "Mmmm."

Judith chuckled. "You can go ahead and pull the pot out and put your mug under the running stream. It'll be strong, but good."

"I think I like my coffee strong." Claire went over to the counter, where the coffee pot sat working hard for the family. She pulled a mug out of the cupboard and did exactly as Judith had suggested.

Once the mug was full, she replaced the pot and added her cream and sugar. It tasted perfect. "I seem to learn more and more about myself every day." Her sigh filled the room.

Judith put the pot in the soapy sink and turned around. "Really? You have a memory?" It was not that she wanted Claire gone, it was that she wanted the poor girl healed enough to remember who she was and who her husband was.

There may have been a little bit of protectiveness for her son, who seemed to be a bit too attracted to the pretty girl. But, she'd never boot the girl out of her house. If anything, she would kick Matthew out to one of the cabins reserved for seasonal workers.

"No, nothing like that. But the taste of this coffee is perfection. I think I do like strong coffee." Her eyes widened, and she gave a sheepish look at her hostess. "I'm sorry. That didn't sound right. I love your coffee no matter what. It's just...well...this is hitting the spot right now." She took another sip and thoroughly enjoyed the hints of hickory and spice mixed with the vanilla creamer and sugar.

Judith chortled. "Honey, don't worry. I know what you meant. Sometimes I do the same. Especially on tough mornings."

"You have tough mornings?" Claire could not imagine that anything went wrong for Judith. She had a wonderful family and a husband who adored her. She had not missed the loving looks they shared when they thought no one was looking.

And last night at the bonfire, she had noticed Mr. and Mrs. Manning holding hands and snuggling up under a shared blanket. They were really cute together.

"Sometimes, getting older is tough." Judith shook her head and fixed herself a cup of coffee. "My body doesn't always do what I want it to. Extra-strong coffee helps when I have a few aches, or didn't get enough sleep."

"Oh." Claire could not remember if she had any of those issues. Of course, she had aches right now, but that was from her accident, whatever it was. She just assumed that once she was healed there would be no more pain. "I'm sorry. You seem like nothing goes wrong. I think you have more energy than I do."

They both laughed and enjoyed a moment of silence, and they took more sips of their coffee.

"I think you haven't been around long enough. Give it a few days. You'll get more energy and I'll have a rough morning. It's bound to happen." The matriarch of the family did not ever complain, but she did have mornings where she wished she could sleep in just a bit.

"Hmmm." Claire nodded and thought for a moment. "When you have one of those mornings, let me know and I'll take over for you." Her cheeks warmed. "That is, if I'm still here."

Judith reached a hand out and rubbed Claire's arm. "I just might take you up on that offer."

"How about I help you with these dishes and then I can fix my own breakfast?" If Judith was talking about bad mornings, Claire thought it was possible she was having one today. If there was anything she could do to help the woman who took her into her home, she would.

"Thank you, dear." Judith sat down and sighed before taking a long sip of her hot coffee.

As Claire worked on finishing the dishes, she promised herself she would help out more around the house while she was there. It was possible Judith was only having a bad day that day. She still needed to pull her weight. And since she felt so much better than even the day before, now was the time to help.

If she continued to heal at this rate, she would be fine before she even went back to see the doctor again. That thought motivated her, and she smiled as she finished up the dishes.

Claire and Judith worked together all morning. They had cleaned the house and had a nice luncheon all set up when the men of the family came in before noon. She had heard people coming and going all morning, probably to get coffee or snacks, but she had not seen anyone during the few times she had been in the kitchen. Most of the morning she was in the living room or family room cleaning. She even cleaned the hall bathroom.

"Claire, lunch is ready," Judith called down the hall when Claire was vacuuming the hallway.

"Be right there!" she called out.

By the time she had put everything away and made her way to the kitchen, everyone was seated with bowls of steaming soup and hot bread in front of them. Judith had made homemade chili and cornbread.

Claire's stomach gurgled and she put a hand to it, hoping no one heard.

Matthew smiled and waved her over. "Don't worry, we all had the same response when we walked in today. Ma's chili and cornbread is a favorite around here."

While Claire felt a little better, it was still embarrassing to have the entire family hear her stomach gurgle as though she had not eaten in days when she'd had a large breakfast of eggs, toast, and bacon. She even ate five pieces of the tasty pork.

However, with all the housework she had done over the

past few hours, she wasn't just exhausted, she was also starving.

The only seat open was the one next to Matthew. When she sat down she smiled at him, and something inside her fluttered. She wasn't sure if it was the fact that she was so hungry, tired, or *him*, but something caused a flurry of butterfly wings to zip around her stomach.

She chastised herself for thinking another man might have given her feelings—she had a husband, after all. Or at the very least, she had a fiancé. Every time she thought about the mysterious missing groom, she thought she could not be married. How could she if she did not even remember him, or the wedding? No, she was convinced they never married.

The rest of lunch flew by with her staying quiet as she ate two helpings of the moist cornbread along with a large bowl of chili topped with cheese.

"Ma, that was perfect," Matthew said as he finished the last of two bowls of chili he had eaten.

"Perfect as always, honey," Mr. Manning said, and smiled at his wife before kissing her cheek and heading back outside.

The rest of the boys followed him, and Claire stood up to help clear the table.

"Oh, don't worry about these, dear. Please, go and lay down for a little while." Judith looked at Claire's face and tsk'd. "You look tired."

Claire felt tired, and she hoped she did not look anywhere near as bad as she felt. "How about I help you clear the table before I take a nap?"

Judith shook her head. "No, please go sleep. I don't need Harper getting after me for working you too hard. Remember, you still need extra rest."

Even though she wanted to help, Claire was glad Judith insisted she lay down. "I'll be out soon to help with dinner."

Judith smiled and began to clear the table, and Claire walked back to her room.

The moment her head hit the pillow, she fell into a deep sleep. Claire did not wake until Judith knocked on her door two hours later.

"Come in," Claire lazily called as she stretched out on the bed.

"I'm so sorry to disturb your sleep, but the sheriff's here. He'd like to ask you some more questions." Judith's head peeked through the door.

Claire sat up quickly. "Oh? Do you think he knows anything?"

Mrs. Manning shook her head. "I honestly don't know. He's in the living room and I'll get you both some sweet tea."

"Okay." Claire jumped out of bed and put her house shoes on before checking to make sure her head was not a rat's nest before leaving the room.

"Sheriff Roscoe, it's good to see you." Claire smiled as she entered the living room and took a seat across from the lawman. She was feeling nervous. If this went the way she hoped, she would know who she was. And hopefully whether she was actually married or still engaged.

"Claire, you're lookin' much better than the last time I saw you." The sheriff put his forearms on his knees and looked Claire up and down. He had been worried about her health, but looking at the girl, he knew she was getting the care she needed.

She chuckled. "I feel much better than the last time I saw you."

"I take it the Mannings are takin' good care of ya?"

Claire nodded and smiled as Judith came in with a tray carrying two tall glasses of tea.

"Thank you, Judith." The sheriff took one of the glasses before taking a long drink.

"Thank you." Claire smiled at her hostess and took a sip before setting the glass down on the side table. She was too nervous and excited to bother with drinking anything. She just wanted to know who she really was. "Do you have any news about me?"

The hopeful look on Claire's face caused the sheriff to clear his throat. "Nothin' yet. We haven't stopped lookin'." The sheriff felt horrible that he did not have any news yet on her family, or her identity. "The only thing we know for certain is that there wasn't a car accident within a twenty-mile radius of where you were found."

Roscoe rubbed the back of his neck. "We've spoken with all the tow companies, and nothin' along that stretch of highway suggests a car went off the side of the road. The state troopers have also been searching, and they've discovered nothing as well."

Claire slouched in her seat, feeling defeated. "Surely someone somewhere knows what happened, right?"

He nodded. "Someone knows something. The fact that there aren't any missing persons reports matching your description does have me worried. But, it could be that you aren't expected anywhere yet."

"Have you checked the airports to see if there was a reservation for a Claire Brown?" Matthew walked into the room staring intently at the sheriff.

He had been outside in the paddock with his horse, Thunder, when he heard the sheriff pull up. After he put his horse away, he came inside to see who had come for a visit.

Roscoe nodded. "We did. Nothing for anyone with the first name of Claire. Brown is too common a name, so we don't know if her fiancé, or husband, flew out. But no one with the last name of Brown missed a flight."

"Rats. I really hoped that would lead to something." Matthew stood off to the side of the sheriff, not wanting to sit down in his dirty jeans and mess up his mother's good furniture.

"So, what's next?" Claire had no clue how to find a missing person, or in her case, find the family of a missing person.

The sheriff sighed. "I'm here to see if you've remembered anything yet."

Defeat settled along her spine. Claire felt tears prick at the backs of her eyes, and she rubbed them. "No. Nothing." She looked up. "Where do we go from here?"

"I think we need to post your picture on social media and see if anyone recognizes you." The sheriff could not bring himself to look into the sad face of the pretty girl. He felt as though he had not done his job and was letting her down. Although, he was not giving up. He would keep looking. Someone had to miss her. They'd be filing a missing persons report soon. He just knew it.

"Alright, if you think that'll help." Claire stood up and waited as Sheriff Roscoe took his cell phone out to take her picture.

She smiled, but it was forced. The idea of posting her picture all over social media asking if anyone knew her embarrassed her. But if it would get her family to call, then she would deal with it.

CHAPTER 12

Once the sheriff left, Matthew took Claire's hand and led her out of the room. "How about we go and see the horses?"

Claire's shoulders straightened, and this time when she smiled it lit up her entire face. "Yes. Thank you."

They walked through the kitchen, and Judith handed them each two carrots with their stalks still attached.

Once they were outside, Claire turned to Matthew. "How'd she know we were going to see the horses?"

He chuckled. "Because around here when anyone is sad, we take treats out to the barn. It works every time."

"Really?"

He nodded. "Yup. Just you wait and see."

Matthew was not wrong. The moment Claire entered the barn, she felt her troubles melt away. Who could not help but smile when surrounded by horses? The strong animals exuded acceptance and love. They did not care what her name was, or who her family was. They only wanted her touch, and probably the treats in their hands.

Claire went straight to Whiskers and rubbed her forehead. "Hey, girl. How ya doing today?"

The horse neighed in response and rubbed her nose against Claire's shoulder.

"You know what's behind my back, don't you, girl?" Claire chuckled and brought out one of the carrots. She laid it flat on her palm and put it under Whiskers' mouth.

The horse snuffled a moment and then lifted the end of the carrot into her mouth and munched on it.

As Whiskers ate her treat, Claire rubbed the horse's mane and felt her worries fly away in the breeze.

An hour later, she and Matthew walked into the kitchen for another cup of coffee.

"See, what'd I tell ya?" Matthew smirked as he poured coffee into two blue mugs.

She nodded. "Okay, I'll admit it this time." Her eyes sparkled, and her smile lit her face like a thousand-watt bulb. Being around the horses had done wonders for her mood.

THE PHOTO on social media had caused a storm, but not the type of storm the sheriff hoped for. Apparently, there were some very skeevy men out there who thought they could claim an amnesiac and no one would question it.

"What's her last name?" The sheriff was on his fifth call with men who claimed Claire was their wife.

"Olson. Her name's Claire Olson and I've been worried sick about her." The man on the phone who claimed to be Claire's husband sounded worried, but it all still sounded so fake.

Once the first call came in, the sheriff thought he had gotten lucky until the man said he was a pig farmer from

Wyoming. He and Claire had been in Montana at a fair. Roscoe did not doubt the man was a pig farmer from Wyoming, but the details about her were all off.

Hoping it was a fluke, the sheriff had been a bit more open to the idea of the second man until he told the sheriff she had been wearing blue jeans, brown boots, and a button-up shirt when she went missing.

After that, the sheriff did not believe anyone.

Mr. Olson was probably the closest one to the right story, but he still did not mention the wedding dress.

AFTER DINNER THAT NIGHT, the sky was streaked with purple, orange, and red clouds. Matthew walked outside and stood on the front patio looking out to the developing storm. He knew at some point during the night, they'd be getting rain. The only question was how much?

When Claire walked out with two tall glasses of iced cold sweet tea, he couldn't help but smile. She motioned for him to join her on the cushioned chairs and he obliged her.

"Thank you, this is perfect." Matthew took a long sip of the tea and sighed. He could get used to nights like this where they sat outside together drinking tea and watching a storm roll in.

Claire pulled her long sweater a bit tighter around her when a cold gust of wind blew through the patio. While it was covered, it wasn't screened in. A quick thought of a screened patio and a sunset rolled through her head. For a split second she wanted to pull on it, but she didn't want the resulting headache, which would only ruin the perfect evening.

Neither of them spoke. They sat there watching the clouds

roll by and Claire listened to the sounds of the crickets as they chirped and moved through the tall grasses around the property.

Matthew was happy his mother had redone the patio furniture last summer with comfortable pillows that made sitting there relaxing and enjoyable. It was one of his favorite places to relax at night before going to bed. The simple nights of watching the sky turn from yellows, light blues, and oranges, to dark blues and midnight purples, then the resulting stars in the pitch-black skies always helped him to sleep better.

Never had he felt so comfortable sitting with another woman and *not* talk. He tried to convince himself it was just friendship that was developing between them, and nothing more. But even he knew it was a weak argument. If he had his choice, they would spend every night like this, together.

"This is beautiful. I bet you sit out here every night and enjoy the peace and beauty of what God created for us." Claire sighed and kept her eyes on Cassiopeia.

"I never understood why Ptolemy named that constellation," he pointed to a zigzag of lines connecting five stars above them, "after a queen."

Claire shook her head. "I honestly don't know. Maybe it was because she was a vain queen and he wanted to take her down a peg or two? It's not a very pretty set of stars, is it? I mean compared to the rest of the night sky." She craned her head one direction and then another looking at the stars and wondering what it would have been like to have a set of them named after her. Not that she was vain, but the idea of her name living on resonated with her at that moment.

It was most likely because she had felt neglected and forgotten. If her family could not be bothered with remembering her, maybe someone else would if she were immortalized in the stars.

It was a silly thought and she knew it. There had to be a rational explanation for why no one was looking for her yet. One thought she had earlier in the day, that came back to haunt her now, was that she had no family. Maybe she was supposed to marry a man and then he ran out on her at the last moment? That could explain why her family was not looking for her, they were not alive anymore.

Even though the idea did not feel right, she did consider it again.

"Hmmm, maybe you're right." Matthew looked intently at the constellation. "I think I like the look of the giant spoon better." He smirked.

"Giant spoon?" Claire's brows rose and lines developed just above the bridge of her nose. "Is that what you call the big dipper?"

"What's a big dipper?" Matthew turned confused eyes on her but he couldn't hold it in any longer and he busted out laughing. "Oh my goodness, the look on your face. You really believed I didn't know what the big dipper was, did you?"

She reached over and slapped his shoulder. "Not funny." But it was. When she joined in on the laughter, her heart lifted and the heaviness of her thoughts fled into the vastness of space.

THE MOMENT CLAIRE woke up on the fourth day, she had a smile on her face. She even got up before her alarm went off. This was the day the Mannings were going to let her ride Whiskers. Not only did she sleep like a baby the night before, she felt like a million dollars.

When she walked into the kitchen earlier than she had made it any day since she'd arrived, Judith turned around, shocked but smiling.

"Claire." Judith looked her guest up and down. "You look like you had a great night of sleep." She knew why Claire was so excited. At dinner the night before, it was all the young woman could talk about. Especially after Harper gave her the go-ahead to ride the next day.

Of course, Nurse Harper had given the entire household a stern warning about Claire taking it easy. Claire did not care as long as she was allowed to sit astride a horse. Her soul screamed for her to get on a horse.

"Surprisingly, I did. And now I'm ready for a ride." She beamed when she accepted a cup of coffee from Judith and went to add her cream and sugar.

"I think you'll want to sit down and have breakfast first. Then you'll need to wait for Matthew to take you out."

"Oh, I know. He told me so many times last night how this was going to play out today." Claire chuckled, remembering how stern Matthew's face was when he warned her about how seriously he took the doctor's and Harper's warnings.

Claire took a sip of her coffee and sighed. "I seriously doubt in my previous life I had such good coffee."

Judith laughed. "What makes you say that?"

She put her cup down and walked over to the cutting board and took over dicing tomatoes and peppers from Judith. "Well, each time I get a cup of your coffee I feel like this is the best cup of coffee I've ever had. I think my taste buds know what they like, even if I can't remember."

"Well, I may be biased, but have ta agree, little lady." Mr. Manning walked in with his sons behind him. He walked over to his wife and gave her a kiss on the cheek.

"You've got about ten minutes to wash up and get back to the table. Or you might be eating cold eggs." Judith whisked a bowl of eggs and added some milk to it before she poured it in the pan.

"Yes, ma'am." Mr. Manning winked at his wife and tipped his hat to Claire.

"You two are so cute." Claire sighed before getting back to her chopping.

"I'm truly blessed. God has been so good to me." Judith smiled off in the distance like a besotted teenager watching the boy she crushed on saunter away.

"Yes, I'd say you are." Claire dumped the chopped vegetables in two pans, took the spatula from Judith, and stirred the contents of each skillet. They were making a Denver omelet scramble. The ham had already warmed up before the eggs were poured in. Since there were so many of them, they needed two giant skillets in order to make enough for everyone to eat at the same time.

In another skillet, Judith finished browning the second batch of hash browns and moved it off the burner and covered it after she turned the lit burner off.

Judith looked at Claire from the corner of her eye, wondering if she should say anything. She had noticed how friendly her son and this young woman had become since she arrived earlier in the week. While she had mentioned something to Matthew, she had not really said anything to Claire.

"What about your husband? Does he look at you the way mine does me?" She hoped the lightness in her voice did not worry Claire or let on that she was worried about Claire getting too close to Matthew. She thought that if she could get Claire to remember that she had a husband, she might take pains to ensure that Matthew did not get too close.

She shrugged. "I wish I could remember. But whenever I

think about him…" Claire trailed off, not really sure how to explain what she felt. She bit her lip and kept her eyes on the skillet of scrambled eggs, ham, and veggies. "Nothing. I don't feel anything other than emptiness."

"Hmmm." Judith considered her words carefully before saying anything else. "Why do you think that is?" She could not imagine ever forgetting that she was married. Even with amnesia, her entire being would *know* she had a husband. But, she'd been married for almost thirty-five years. Had she lost her memory the day of her wedding, maybe she would not remember.

Claire shrugged. She did not want to think too hard because she did not want a headache to come on and ruin her ride. Although, the headaches were fewer and fewer each day.

The idea of her husband being out there, somewhere, had hurt. No one was looking for her, and she wondered what that meant about him, and her. Didn't he love her? Even if he did not love her, why wasn't he looking?

"I think there's something else going on. I doubt there was a wedding. I mean, I was found on Tuesday night. Who has a wedding on a Tuesday?" Claire had wondered if maybe she disappeared after trying on a wedding dress. Maybe there was not even a fiancé out there. That could explain why no one was looking for her.

Judith stopped with a serving dish in her hand and looked at Claire. "Huh, I hadn't thought of that. But a Tuesday wedding is not completely unheard of. Or, maybe you had been out there on the road since Sunday? You were dehydrated and injured. Who knows how long you were out there for."

A timer dinged, signaling the toast was done. After Judith put the dish on the table, she walked over to the sideboard where she had two large toaster ovens. She pulled the toast out and stacked it on a plate and put in another eight pieces of toast between the two little ovens.

Claire quirked her lips and thought about it. "If I was getting married on Sunday, that just makes it all that much worse. Where's my family? Why isn't there a missing persons report for a Claire anywhere near here? My last name may not be Brown, but I feel like Claire is my name." That was about the only thing that felt right. Well, that and her boots.

A brow raised on Judith's forehead and she moved to put the serving dish with the hash browns on the table. "I hope you weren't out there that long, injured and all alone." She shivered. The thought of Claire being all alone on the road, and no one stopping to help her, caused all the hair on her arms to raise. "I doubt you were out on the road that long. Humanity might not be as good as it once was, but a woman bleeding in a dirty and torn wedding dress walking along the road in Montana would have caused someone to stop."

"Someone did stop." Claire tilted her head and gave Judith a knowing look.

"Someone besides my son. He couldn't be the first one to have seen you along the side of the road. Especially if you were out there for days."

Claire turned off both burners and moved the skillets of food to a serving dish. "Maybe. But what if I was walking through the brush and trees for days and that was the first time I had made it to a road?" She had not really thought about where she had been. All she could remember was waking up in the arms of a cowboy who walked her to his truck. Then she was in the clinic. She had no memory before Matthew showed up.

Matthew had heard what they were discussing, and for a

moment, rage flared through him at the thought that anyone would pass her on the road and not stop to help. But then he thought about how she looked. "I agree with Claire. I think whatever happened was recent. While the blood had stopped flowin', it was fresh. She wasn't burnt from the sun. And Ma's right: no one would have driven by without stopping to help."

Both women in the kitchen jumped.

Claire put a hand over her heart. "You shouldn't sneak up on women in the kitchen when they're cooking. I could have dropped a plate and you wouldn't have breakfast."

He chuckled. "I didn't sneak up on you. You were so engrossed in your conversation you missed the loud thunkin' of my boots poundin' on the wooden floor."

Claire chuckled and shook her head. "Maybe." She had been deep in thought.

"What do you say we table this conversation for later and get breakfast going?" Judith asked when she put the butter and jam on the table and took her seat.

The rest of the family filed in and took their seats. The loud conversations about what each of the Manning men were up to for the day took over, and soon they had prayed over the food and everyone dug in.

After Claire helped to clear the table, Matthew led her out to the barn. She would normally insist on helping Judith do the dishes, but with a horse waiting on her, she was not going to argue.

"I can't believe I *finally* get to ride!" Claire squealed before they entered the barn.

She felt like a giddy kid going to her first carnival. Or rodeo. A flash of memory flew through her mind, and a sharp pain caused her to stop and put a hand to her temple. Then she bent over and rubbed both temples as she gritted her teeth.

"Claire, what's wrong?" Worry consumed him, and he hoped he had not pressed her too far too fast. But she had not even gotten on the horse yet.

She put a hand up. "Wait, it'll pass." After a few deep breaths, she stood up straight. Her eyes were still closed and she took deep, ragged breaths in through her nose and out her mouth.

Matthew stood there with his hands fisted at his sides. He wanted to do something, but he knew there was nothing he could do. She had to get through the pain. For a moment he wondered if she needed medicine, but then remembered seeing her take a glass of water and two pills at breakfast. It was too soon for more Advil.

Once her breathing slowed and she felt the pain ease away, she opened her eyes. "Sorry about that." Her cheeks were tinged with pink.

"Don't be sorry. I should be sorry. I shouldn't have pressed for you to ride so soon." He knew without a shadow of a doubt that she was a horsewoman. He had thought riding would bring back memories, but he had not counted on the headaches. In the past two days, he had not witnessed her having a single bit of pain. Which made him think that all was fine.

However, he should have known that when memories came back, she would have pain.

She put a hand up. "Don't. It's not your fault. I wanted this just as badly as you, if not more. I should have prepared myself for the memory to come and the pain that would inevitably accompany it."

"A memory? What was it?" He relaxed now that she was

no longer in obvious pain, and he even hoped she would get something good out of this experience.

"I'm not quite sure, but I think I remembered something from childhood." She looked at him and furrowed her brow. "Maybe I went to a rodeo?"

His eyes opened wide, and a slow smile spread across his face. "That's great. Were you in the stands, or on a horse?"

"I think I was on a horse." While she wanted to explore that memory, she knew better than to force it out. Part of a memory was good, and she would have to accept that for now.

He slapped his thigh. "Well, what do ya know! You're probably a rodeo star. Maybe you were..." He stopped his train of thought. He could not go there and get his hopes up. No, she may be a good horsewoman, but there was not a horse out there anywhere near her when he found her.

Hope entered her eyes. "Maybe I was what? Doing a rodeo show and somehow that dress was a costume?" She bit the inside of her cheek as she thought about it. While it sounded exciting, it did not *feel* right. However, that would explain her first name inside the dress, just not the strange-feeling last name.

They both shook their heads at the same time. "Nah, that's too farfetched." While Matthew wished it were true, he knew it could not be. Had she been missing from a rodeo, someone would have reported her by now.

"Well, should we saddle up?" She put a brave face on and strode to where she knew Matthew kept the saddles. Hope began to fill her heart again as she realized that she'd had a memory come back. She had not even saddled the horse yet, and she was already starting to get memories. Who knew how many more would come once she was out riding?

That thought also sent dread through her spine. The last

thing she needed was to have Matthew worry about her headaches and demand they go back right away. She could not have him cutting off her rides. She would have to do whatever she could to stop memories from surfacing while she rode. Getting in a saddle was more important to her than getting her memory back.

At least for today.

CHAPTER 13

They had only ridden for an hour, and Claire was given a more detailed tour of the land than what Matthew could have given her on foot the other day. While she was not ready to go back in yet, she was extremely happy to have had that small amount of time on Whiskers.

"When can we go back out again?" Her words sounded breathless to her, and she hoped Matthew had not picked up on it. He might think she was exhausted. She was tired, but not too much.

Matthew dismounted from his horse, Thunder, and smiled as he walked toward Claire. Her face beamed, and her eyes shone from the excitement she felt from the ride. "I take it you enjoyed yourself?" He could not help but smirk.

The cowboy knew that Claire would love riding. She gave off an air of being an accomplished horsewoman even before she sat astride the horse. It was evident every time they saw the horses together. Today only proved what he already suspected. And he was very glad to have been the one to help her learn more about herself.

"Yes, and next time can we stay out longer?" She sighed

and looked out to the pastures behind the barn and wished they were not already back at the ranch house. If he'd have let her, she would have been out all day riding. A picnic might be nice next time.

His deep chuckle so near her brought her out of her fantasy. "Oh, sorry. Yes, I should probably dismount so we can get the horses rubbed down and fed." She smiled and started to get off the horse on her own when he stilled her with his hands on her waist.

She sucked in a quick breath and her eyes widened from the contact. That feeling she'd had the other day returned, and the butterflies went into overdrive.

Matthew saw the look of surprise on Claire's face, and he returned it. The shock he felt when he touched her so intimately surprised him. It was his duty to help her down; she was still too weak to allow her to dismount on her own. But, he couldn't take his eyes off hers. When they darkened, he knew he was in big trouble.

When he was sure he had a good grip on her hips, he pulled her off the horse. The poor filly could not have weighed more than a wet blanket. She came right off and into his arms. The heat generated between them both at an alarming rate, and he lost all control.

Slowly, so very slowly as not to scare her away, his head dipped, and his eyes moved to her lips.

She licked her lips in anticipation, and she no longer had butterflies flitting about her stomach. Now it was a full-on stampede, and she had nowhere to go. Not that she wanted out of his way. No, she wanted his lips on hers more than she wanted water or air.

His warm breath against her skin caused her to shiver, and slowly she moved her hands up from where they had been on his shoulders to behind his neck. Her eyes flittered, and she took in his delicious scent of leather, spice, and horse. She had no idea that horse could smell so intoxicating. But mixed with his own personal scent, it was the best thing in the world.

He was less than an inch away from kissing her when her eyes closed and stayed closed. His eyes took in the beauty of her nose, the soft lashes on her eyes, and how her lips slowly parted in anticipation of his.

"Hey, how was…" Mark stopped dead in his tracks and watched in horror as his big brother was about to kiss a married woman. Or at least, someone they thought might be married. "Um… I think Ma needs Claire's help."

Mark was not about to let his brother make such a huge mistake. While his mother had not actually asked for Claire, he knew she'd be very happy to have the cowgirl in her kitchen if it meant saving her oldest son from making the biggest mistake of his life.

The couple jumped apart, and Claire turned away from Mark. She felt the burn on her cheeks as she realized too late what had almost happened. Even if she wanted it more than getting her memory back, she could not do that to him, or to whomever she might be married to. It did not matter that he wasn't looking for her; she still had an obligation to keep her vows, if they were married.

Matthew cleared his throat and rubbed a hand down his face. He could not believe he'd almost kissed a married woman. That could not happen. It did not matter if she didn't know who she was, he knew she was most likely married. And if not quite married, she was most certainly engaged. After he blew out a long breath, he turned to his brother.

"What did Ma want?" He knew Mark had said something about his mother, but he could not think well enough to remember what his brother said.

Mark still stood right in the entrance to the barn, where he had found the couple almost kissing. "Ahh, I think she needs help in the kitchen." He had not seen his mother, or even been asked to find either of them. He had only seen them come back and wanted to know how the ride went. Apparently, it went too well.

"Right. Of course. Excuse me, I'll go and help her right away." Claire kept her head down as she passed both cowboys. She had no desire for either of them to see her embarrassment.

As she walked away, she mentally kicked herself for not being more careful. She knew she was attracted to the cowboy, but it was not possible. He was off-limits. Or more accurately, *she* was off-limits.

When she was out of earshot, Mark punched his brother's shoulder. "What were you thinkin', man? She's a married woman." Angered seethed out of his words. The big brother he had always idolized was about to commit adultery. How had his brother fallen so far, so fast?

Matthew ran a shaky hand through his messy hair. "I don't know. The entire time we were out ridin' we kept it platonic. We laughed and talked, but there was nothin' untoward 'bout it all." He sighed. "But when I went to help her down…" He slapped his thigh and grabbed Thunder's reins to walk him back to his stall.

Mark took Whiskers' reins and followed. "When you helped her down, what?"

Matthew had to think about what he wanted to say. He knew he had messed up, big time. If his father had been the one to find them, he probably would have kicked him out and told him not to come back until he had cleaned himself up. And Matthew would not have blamed him, either. Shoot, he was not sure if Mark wouldn't do it. He deserved to be kicked out and left to fend for himself while he made amends and got right with God.

"Oh Lord, what have I done?" He began to pray in earnest, but was stopped by a hand on his shoulder. He jumped and turned around to see a stern-looking, younger version of his father.

"Matthew, was it just a fluke? Or do you have real feelings for the woman?" The question from his younger brother took him off guard.

His head drooped, and shame flooded his system. "I think I have real feelings."

"What are you going to do?" The tone in Mark's voice changed to pity, which only caused Matthew to feel even worse.

He did not deserve his brother's pity. He deserved anger and scorn.

CHAPTER 14

The next morning brought clarity—and hopefully discipline—for Claire. She made it up in time to help set the table for breakfast and joined the family as they sat down to pray for the bounty God had given them.

When they were about halfway through breakfast, Matthew looked to Claire. "How 'bout you help me this morning with fixin' that fence line we saw yesterday?"

"I thought you were going to let that old bull have a way to visit his girlfriends?" Claire chuckled and took a bite of toast with brambleberry jam.

The men around the table chuckled and told various stories of catching the old bull in their pastures with their cows.

"I think we might want to consider putting in a gate and only letting Mr. Johnson's bull come for visits on special occasions," Mr. Manning offered.

Matthew nodded. "I agree. We need to keep a good, strong fence line up to ensure there aren't too many crossovers."

"Crossovers?" Claire's confused look prompted Matthew to explain.

"If the fence is down, our cows could go over into the Johnson pastures, and their cows could come over in our own." Matthew stopped long enough to take a sip of his coffee.

But he was not quick enough, because Mark took over the explanation. "If the cows don't have a fence, they think the land is theirs to graze on. While we have a good relationship with Mr. Johnson, it can be a pain to go and look in someone else's land for our own cattle, and vice versa. We don't need to add anything that might cause difficulty between our two ranches."

"Ah, I see." Claire knew they all branded their own cattle, but with hundreds, if not thousands, of acres between the two ranches, it could be difficult to find your own cows if they wandered too far.

"Would I get to ride Whiskers out to the fence line?" Claire was up for anything if it involved riding a horse.

"I was thinking something a little more exciting." Matthew grinned and kept the mode of travel to himself.

When Mark started to spill the beans, Matthew slapped his shoulder and shook his head.

"Alright, boys. You know the rules." Judith waggled a finger at her boys and gave them a stern look.

"Yes, Ma," they both responded right away.

While they were not fighting, they were not allowed to even slap each other in the house, and most certainly not at the table. Their parents had both instilled in them from a very young age no fighting in the house, and no horsing around at the table.

Mark looked down at his plate and stayed quiet as he finished his breakfast.

John offered to help his mother clean the table and do dishes so that Claire could go and help Matthew mend the fence.

The pair walked outside without a word and headed toward the barn. When they were a few feet away, Matthew veered to the side and Claire stopped walking abruptly.

"Where are you going?" She pointed to the barn and furrowed her brows. She thought they were going to get the horses and head out to fix the fence.

He smiled and waved for her to follow. "Come on, I've got a surprise for you."

"A surprise?" She was not sure if she liked surprises, but at that moment, she did. Giddiness engulfed her as she practically ran to catch up to the tall cowboy.

When they approached an outbuilding that looked more like a small garage than a barn, she stopped and watched Matthew open the roll-top door.

"Come on." He winked and waved at Claire to follow him.

It was dark inside the building, until Matthew flipped a switched. When the light bathed the room in color, she gasped. Across the floor sat several four-wheelers.

"ATVs?" She clapped her hands together and knew without a shadow of a doubt, she was a rancher. Everything about this place screamed comfort and home to her. While she could not call up a memory of riding one of them, she figured it would be like riding a bike and it would all come back to her without any problems.

"I love it!" she exclaimed as she ran up to the red four-wheeler and put her hands on the handlebar once she sat down.

"Whoa now, we don't know if you can ride them, so for today we're going to share the ride. When we're done, I'll let you drive if you feel comfortable." He chuckled and loved that she was so excited over something as simple as a piece of ranch equipment.

And equipment it was. Even though the family did have many days where they rode the ATVs for fun, they were necessary for getting to parts of the ranch the trucks could not get to as easily as a smaller vehicle.

They were also much better for hauling equipment, such as long fence posts and wire. While the trailer they hooked up to the back of the largest ATV could be used to haul a sick cow or a calf that needed extra help getting back to the barn, it was almost exclusively used for mending fences or hauling dirt to cover up holes.

"Ah, come on. I know I can ride these." She put her hands together in a pleading motion and wanted to be able to ride one without being so close to Matthew. After their almost-kiss the day before, she needed to keep a physical distance from the yummy cowboy.

He shook his head. "No way. It's dangerous if ya don't know what you're doing. I'm not goin' t' be the one who gets you hurt, again." He held his hands up. "Do you know what my ma would do to me if you got hurt on my watch?" A shiver made its way down his spine.

Claire laughed. "Oh, come on. Your mom is sweet. She wouldn't hurt you."

Matthew shook his head. "You didn't grow up with her. As a kid, I always wanted my pa to do the punishin'. While it hurt, it was much faster and easier to take than hers."

Real fear entered Matthew's eyes, and Claire wondered what in the world his mom could have done to him as a kid. She did not seem like the type to abuse her kids.

When Matthew noted the confusion on Claire's face, he sighed. "When we were kids, if Ma got upset with us she'd put us on the porch for all meals and not talk to us 'till after dinner. Kinda like a cowboy timeout. The look she gave us always caused more pain then a spanking did. Knowing I disappointed my Ma was the worst thing ever."

"Wow, you must really love and respect your mother to feel so horrible when you disappointed her." She wondered how she was punished as a kid and if she felt for her mom the way Matthew obviously did for his.

A pain shot through her chest, and she winced. Did she have a loving mother she respected more than anything? She sure hoped so.

When Matthew had a helmet in his hand, he turned to her and grinned. "Come on, let's get goin'. We need to hurry up if we wanna get back in time to shower and join Elizabeth and her crew in Bozeman later today."

Claire had been looking forward to helping feed the homeless and seeing what Elizabeth had been talking about earlier in the week when she said the women needed their help. Judith had spoken about a few women they had helped get back on their feet and head home to their families.

Not for the first time, Claire wondered what type of woman she was. Did she help the needy back home? Was there some sort of charity she was involved with? She hoped she did something to help others.

Claire took the helmet from his hands and went to put it on. She winced once the helmet was down around her head and tried to pull the side away that hurt her head.

"Oh, I'm sorry, Claire. I completely forgot about your injury. If you want to follow me on Whiskers, we can do that. But I need to ride the ATV since I need the supplies and tools that I'll pull behind it." He wondered if maybe it would be better for his heart to have her on a horse instead of behind him on the seat with her arms wrapped around his middle.

On second thought, he hoped she would choose the horse. It was definitely the better choice.

"No, no. I'll be fine. I just needed to move the helmet around into a better position, that's all." She smiled and adjusted the chin strap.

Great, he was in trouble.

Matthew put on his helmet and rolled the small trailer outside the shed and then went back in and started up the ATV before taking it outside to hook up to the trailer. "Alright, get on the seat behind me and hold on tight. But you have to let me know if you're in pain if the jostling is too much, or the helmet is too tight."

She grinned. "No way. This is going to be awesome."

"I'm serious, Claire. I'll drive at a snail's pace if you don't promise to tell me if you're hurting. I don't want to add to your aches and pains. And I certainly don't want to do anything that could cause you more pain." He also did not want to do anything to keep her from getting her memory back. Well, that was not completely true. While he did not want to hurt her, the little devil on his shoulder told him to keep her to himself and ensure she never got her memory back. That way she would be all his. He shook his head and prayed for strength.

When she wrapped her arms around him, Matthew's hand hit the gas a bit too hard and he jerked them forward. The ATV stuttered and then stalled. It was a good thing she could not see his face. He felt the warmth cover his neck and face so fast, he knew his entire face had to be red.

He had not stalled out a four-wheeler since he first learned how to ride as a kid. But when she touched his waist and leaned against him, he caught a whiff of her clean, fresh scent and images of cut grass, lavender fields, and something sweet flitted through his mind. He could not help it.

She was going to be the death of him. He just knew he would be having a heart attack any day now.

"Sorry 'bout that." He cleared his throat of the frog trying to hop out and started the machine again. This time, he eased them out of the area and back toward the fence line in the back of the property along the line with Mr. Johnson.

Even though they were going slow enough that they could have chatted if they yelled over the sounds of the engine, both stayed quiet.

Claire could not believe she was this close to Matthew. When he first suggested she ride Whiskers out, she should have accepted. Had she known what holding onto him would do to her heart, she would have jumped at the chance to keep a physical distance between them.

It was all she could do to keep her heart in her chest, it was beating so hard. She hoped he could not feel the pounding of her heart against his back.

The moment they finally stopped, she jumped off the ATV as fast as humanly possible and took her helmet off. Claire could not bring herself to look at the man who made her feel things she should not.

"Okay." Matthew felt like he had to say something; the silence was awkward for the first time, and he could not focus. Without knowing what to say, he went to the fence and looked at the two loose posts. "We'll need to replace 'em both and set new holes."

Matthew moved one of the posts around in its hole and noted that the dirt was wet, and he could not get the dirt to dry in time for just a quick replacement. He would need to dig a new hole and set a new post. The one in that hole should have lasted longer, but it looked to be on its last leg.

Claire walked over to look at the problem and narrowed her eyes. "Why's the ground wet right there, but not all over?" She knew it had not rained in a couple days, so the ground should have been dry.

Matthew leaned down, and after he put on his gloves he picked up some of the dirt. When the acrid scent hit his nose, he threw it down and almost gagged. "Oh, that's bad." He stood up and wiped his dirty glove on the top of the post.

"What?" Claire started to lean over to get a whiff herself when she felt a hand on her arm pulling her back up.

He shook his head. "Trust me, you don't want to smell it."

Claire laughed, and a remnant of joke—maybe something from when she was a kid?—flitted through her mind and out of her mouth without even knowing it. "Whoever smelt it, dealt it."

Her eyes widened like saucers when she realized she had vocalized the words running through her memory.

Matthew busted up laughing, almost bending over. "Sorry, honey. I most certainly did not deal that one." He pointed to a lump in the distance.

She turned around and saw the ornery ol' bull. With furrowed brows, she turned back to Matthew. "Huh? I don't get it."

"Something, most likely that ol' bull, released their bladder here." Matthew considered why he would pee on the fence, specifically the fence post, and laughed. "Man, that ol' bull is too smart for our own good."

When he saw the confused look on Claire's face, he stopped laughing and looked back at the post. "His urine helped to weaken the post's position in the dirt."

She blinked a few times and looked between the bull and the fence post. "But…that would take a lot of urine to get the dirt wet enough to push the post loose."

"The rain from the other day probably did most of the work, and he just kept peeing on it and pushing against the fence line. This must be how he always finds a way to get in." He shook his head and realized they were going to have to find a way to outsmart a bull. He had never thought outsmarting a bull would be an issue.

"Seriously?" Claire chuckled and looked around to see if there was a camera focused on them. Surely this was one of those hidden camera shows and they were being punked. "Well, I guess you know now how he does it." She put her hands on her hips. "So, what do we do now?"

He rubbed his chin and nodded. "We still have to fix the fence." Matthew walked over to the small trailer holding fence-mending supplies and grabbed a shovel, post driver, and a fresh post.

Claire walked over and grabbed a pair of gloves out of the tool chest. "Alright, what do I do?"

"You? Stand there an' look pretty." He waggled his brows and grinned.

She slapped his arm like she'd seen his brothers do to each other, although not nearly as hard, and said, "Alright, mister. You better be nice or I'll cut the fence and let that ol' bull in to see his lady friends."

"You wouldn't dare." He knew she would not. Or at least, he hoped she would not. He could fix a cut fence, but it would take a lot longer than they had. Actually, they would most likely be late after they fixed both posts.

She tilted her head and hummed. "Don't test me. I'm not rightly sure what I'd do."

He laughed and nodded. "Fair 'nough. Why don't you help me by holding the wire back while I dig a new hole?"

"You got it, boss."

They had been working together for less than ten minutes when they heard a noise.

Matthew stopped what he was doing and looked back

behind them. Two horses were coming pretty quickly to their location. "Ah, the cavalry is here."

"Hey, bro. How's it goin'?" Mark hopped down off his horse and grinned at Claire before taking in the scene before him.

John dismounted and tipped his hat at Claire.

She nodded in response.

"We've come to save the day." Mark waved his arms around and took a bow.

"Thanks, but I think we've got it in hand." Matthew shook his head and went back to digging his hole.

"Ah, but will you have it done in time to join Elizabeth and the rest of the ladies?" Mark suggestively waggled his brows.

"I take it you have a good reason to want to join this week?" Normally they only went once, maybe twice a month. But for some reason Elizabeth had called them the night before and asked if they wanted to join her Saturday afternoon. She said it would be a quick trip. She felt a strong desire to head up to Bozeman; one of the ladies was on her heart.

When someone was on Elizabeth's heart, it usually meant they needed some extra attention, so everyone was more than happy to join her when they could.

"Maybe." Mark smirked.

John clucked his tongue and shook his head. "You know he does." He grinned at his brother. "I think there's a certain someone he's keen to spend time with today."

"Who, me? Nah, I just want to make sure our sister stays safe." He winked at Matthew and put his gloves on to help.

When they were done fixing both fence posts, they all headed back to the house.

While Claire was on the back of the ATV with Matthew

heading home, she did not feel as though the ride was nearly as intense as when they were alone. Maybe having others around would help keep her heart in check.

It certainly could not hurt.

When Claire entered the kitchen, she stopped short as she noticed a stranger sitting at the table with Judith drinking tea.

Judith stood up and waved for Claire to join them. "Claire, you have a visitor."

Lines etched Claire's almost flawless forehead as she stared in confusion at the man she did not think she had ever met.

"You don't recognize me?" The man stood up and reached for her hands, but pulled back when he saw the confusion on her face. "Claire, darling. It's me—Scott, your husband."

CHAPTER 15

I t could not be. She had no feelings for this man or memories of him. When she had prepared to ride Whiskers earlier, memories began to return. She thought for sure if her husband ever found her, she would have the same experience. Wouldn't she?

"Here, you need to sit." He helped her into one of the chairs at the table.

Scott took a seat next to her.

She felt all the blood drain out of her face and her head felt funny. Was she going to faint? Claire was not sure if she was a fainter, but she did not think so. But what did she know? If this man was her husband and she did not have an inkling of recognition for him, what did she know? Plus, with her almost-kiss moments earlier, she knew she was really off-kilter.

But what about the headaches? Maybe if she tried to remember him, she would get a headache and then see a glimpse of him? Even though she did not want a headache, she needed to try to remember this man.

Judith poured her a tall glass of iced sweet tea and handed it to her.

Claire took a long drink and out of the corner of her eye, she looked the man up and down as best she could. He was not bad looking, but she did not get all flittery looking at him like she did when she looked at... *No*, she scolded herself. She was a married woman. Proof was sitting next to her. She could not think of *him* again.

The man next to her was tall, maybe just under six feet. He had dark-blonde hair and was thin. He did not look like someone who worked a ranch. Not like the Manning men. But he was not malnourished, either. He just had a smaller frame. For all she knew, he had muscles under his long-sleeved, button-down shirt. He was never going to win a bodybuilding contest, but did that really matter?

If she married him, he must be a nice man.

She could not tell the color of his eyes from this angle. Claire put the half-empty glass down and turned in her seat to fully look at the man claiming to be her husband. "Why?"

His brows furrowed and he tilted his head. "Why what?"

"Why didn't you put out a missing persons report on me?" That had been her biggest question this entire time. Why hadn't anyone been out looking for her?

"We fought..." He gave her a sheepish look before turning his gaze on Judith. "Mrs. Manning, could you give us a few moments? I'd like to speak with my wife in private."

Claire gulped. She was not sure she wanted to be alone with the man.

Judith narrowed her eyes and crossed her arms over her chest. "No. I'm not leaving Claire alone with a stranger."

His nostrils flared, and he stood up abruptly. "I'm not a stranger. She's my wife."

"Claire, do you remember this man?" Judith's terse words caused Claire to look about the room nervously.

Claire was not sure who he was, but she did know she felt uncomfortable and did not want to be alone with the man.

"Claire, tell this woman you're fine," Scott ordered.

But she was not fine. And if this was what the man was like, it was no wonder she ran. She shook her head. Since she had woken up in the clinic, she had not known true fear. Not until now. She scooted her chair out and stood up.

"No. You can answer my questions in front of Judith. Or leave." Where she got the courage to stand up to this man, she did not know. But she was not going to be bullied and pushed into a corner by any man, even if he *might* be her husband.

With the way he was acting, she was not even sure he was telling the truth. Another thought hit her, and she wondered if he might *not* be her husband, but one of those crazy men she had heard was asking around about her.

Claire narrowed her eyes and took a few steps closer to Judith. "What was I wearing when I disappeared?" Runaway brides might be a popular trope in books and movies, but they were not real. There was no way he would come up with the right answer.

A smirk crossed his face. "Your wedding dress." He crossed his arms over his chest and a look of triumph took over as her smug face fell.

There was no way he could have known that, unless… "Where's my wedding ring?"

Scott pulled a simple gold band out of his pocket and handed it to her. She put it on, but it was too large for her slender fingers.

He nodded and smiled. "That's why you weren't wearing it. Once we were married, you took it off and put it down so you would not lose it. We were going to have it resized when we got back from our honeymoon."

Her face fell, and she feared she might actually be married to this horrible creature standing in front of her. How else would he know those details?

Scott took the time to look his wife up and down. She was breathtaking, even with the fear etched into her features. And those boots… He smiled. "I see you're still wearing my gift to you." Scott nodded at her feet.

She raised a foot and looked from the boot to her husband. "You gave me these?"

He nodded. "It was an engagement present. You wore them every day, even if they didn't match your outfit, and insisted you wear them for our ceremony."

Triumph crossed his face. He had her now.

Judith put a hand to her mouth. Too many details. This man knew too much about Claire. But he was a brute, she was sure of that.

He turned to Mrs. Manning again. "Now, would you please give us some privacy? We need to talk."

Claire hung her head.

Judith was not sure what to do, but if he was her husband, she had no right to get in the middle. Unless he was about to hurt her. She noticed her cell phone on the counter by the sink and grabbed it. "I'll be in the other room. Holler if you need anything at all, Claire."

She did not wait for a response. Instead, she headed into the living room and shot out a text to her entire family before she even made it to her chair. This was too important to leave to chance. While Judith doubted the man would do anything other than yell at his wife while they were there, she could not be sure.

Once she was seated, she felt antsy and got up to pace the

room while she waited for her reinforcements.

"How'd you find me?" The soft voice that came out of Claire's mouth did not sound like her. It was her voice, but it sounded so defeated, even to her. All she could do was hope and pray that this man was not as mean as she feared.

"The picture of you on social media." He pulled out his phone and held the picture up for her to see. He pointed to the wall behind Claire.

She had to squint and then put her fingers on the screen to expand the picture. Behind her was a picture of the Triple J Ranch and the Manning family.

"Everyone in this state, and probably the surrounding states, knows who the Mannings are." He took his phone back and put it in his pocket.

She nodded. "Why did we fight? Why would I run away from you on our wedding day?" Claire hoped she was not the sort to leave her husband on their wedding day for no good reason. But it was looking like she was the sort.

He sighed. "Do we really need to discuss this now? I would much rather we leave and go home. We can talk about it when we're truly alone."

"No. Claire's not leaving until you prove you're her husband." A tall, imposing figure stood in the doorway to the kitchen with fisted hands at his sides.

When Matthew had received the text from his mom via the emergency group text, he ran immediately to the kitchen without even checking on his ma first. Seeing as how the man wanted to take Claire away immediately, he was glad he had.

Scott sneered and looked Matthew up and down. "She's *my* wife. If I want her to leave with me now, she will."

Claire wrung her hands and stood between the two men. No way was she going to let them fight over her.

Matthew took two steps and was directly behind Claire.

The warmth from his body gave her strength. Strength she needed.

She was not ready to leave, either.

"Matthew's right. If you really are my husband, prove it." She straightened her shoulders and waited.

Scott arched a brow. "Seriously? Him?" He pointed to Matthew. "You haven't even been here a week and you've already cheated on me with him?"

Claire blanched and stuttered. "I have...not! I would never, *ever* cheat on my husband." She wanted to add, *no matter how vile he was*. But she kept that to herself. To punctuate her point, she stomped once on the kitchen floor.

Matthew put his hands on her shoulders and held her in place when she tried to move away. "Sir, I suggest you check yourself. This is my home, and Claire is our guest. If she really is your wife, you shouldn't have any problems proving it."

Scott smirked and pulled out the wedding band he had put back in his pocket. "My wife's wedding ring." He held it between his thumb and forefinger in front of his face. The triumph he felt was written all over his face.

Matthew eyed the ring. "A bland ring doesn't prove anythin'."

"Claire, tell him I'm your husband so we can get going. We have a six-hour drive ahead of us." Scott's exasperated tone infuriated Matthew.

"She's not leaving until the sheriff interviews you." Now it was Matthew's turn to smirk.

Claire lifted a hand. "Uh, I think I can speak for myself." Claire pulled out of Matthew's hands and stood to his side. "I have a lot of questions, not to mention a doctor's appointment on Monday that I'm not going to miss."

She was not sure where that excuse came from, but it

sounded legit. In two more days she was to see her doctor for a follow-up. Hopefully he could shed some light on this situation.

While they all stood there staring at each other, she tried to remember the man in front of her. He had brown eyes, but they did not cause anything in her to stir, not even the beginnings of a headache. Nothing about him felt right, or familiar.

She narrowed her eyes at the ring in her *husband's* hand. "And that doesn't fit me."

Matthew stiffened. "That's not your ring?"

While it was true he didn't know Claire well, he was confident he would have known to buy a smaller-sized ring if she were his intended. And something a bit flashier than a plain gold band. Not that there was anything wrong with it, but Claire did not seem the type to want only a simple band. She seemed more like the diamond-and-platinum band kind of cowgirl.

She shook her head, and it was her turn to look triumphant.

Scott threw his hands in the air. "It was my mother's ring. We were going to get it sized after the honeymoon."

The air might have deflated a little bit from Claire's sails, but she was still confident she would not have wanted to marry the brute who stood in front of her.

Matthew, on the other hand, saw the logic in the ring not fitting Claire if it was a family ring. He could not exactly fault the man for not having it sized before the wedding.

Mr. and Mrs. Manning walked into the kitchen with the rest of their sons who were on the ranch that day. Luke was the only one missing, as he had been in town to have lunch with his girlfriend, Callie.

John, who was normally very quiet, had a hard edge to

him as he got up close to Scott. "How do we know you're Claire's husband?"

A string of expletives left Scott's mouth. "Why do you all keep asking me that? I think I've explained myself as well as I'm going to. She's my wife, not yours." He eyed Matthew and then looked around at all the stern faces watching him.

"Sir, it would behoove you to watch your language around ladies. We don't take kindly to that sort of talk 'round here." Mr. Manning walked to stand in front of his wife, as if to protect her from the nasty words coming out of the vile man's mouth.

Scott rolled his eyes. "Please forgive me." He ran a hand down his clean-shaven face. "This has been a very trying time and I just want to take my wife and go home."

Mark looked between Claire and Scott and shook his head. "The sheriff will be here shortly. She can't leave until he gives her the all-clear. This became a police matter once we found her unconscious on the side of the road."

"Speaking of which," a stern voice said when he walked into the room. The sheriff had been only two ranches away when he got the call from his old friend, Caleb Manning, about Claire's husband showing up out of the blue. "Why didn't you come to the sheriff's station first?"

The lawman had his Stetson in one hand and the other relaxed on his service revolver.

CHAPTER 16

J udith Manning, who never let guests stand long in her
  kitchen, walked around her husband. "Gentlemen, why
  don't you all go and take a seat in the living room?
Claire and I will fix iced tea and bring it out."

The tension had ratcheted up at least twenty degrees when
the sheriff entered the room, and no matter the situation
Judith was not going to forget her manners or let a brawl
break out in her kitchen.

"Good idea, dear." Mr. Manning smiled at his wife and
squeezed her shoulder as he guided the men into the living
room.

When the Manning men made their way into the other
room, they all seemed to know exactly where to sit to ensure
that Scott did not have a chance to sit next to Claire. The only
open spaces were two easy chairs and the spot on the sofa
next to Caleb. His wife would take that seat when she came
back in the room.

The sheriff stood at the window and eyed the stranger.
"Let's start with how you got here and who, exactly, you are."

With all eyes on him, Scott felt the heat of the day settle

on him and a few drops of sweat slowly made their way down his back. He had been around enough lawmen to know that all he had to do was believe what he was selling and he would get away with it. If none of the big city cops ever busted him, this backwater sheriff would never sniff him out.

"My name is Scott Shelling." He knew enough to keep to basics and the truth as much as possible. "I saw the post on social media about my wife and rushed here the moment I realized where she was."

He shook his head and looked down at his hands. They trembled from his nerves, but he knew that only made him seem more believable.

"I didn't think to go to the sheriff's office. All I wanted was to make sure my wife was safe. Now all I want is to take her back to our home and help her get her memory back." Well, that last bit was not even close to the truth, but it sounded good. If he was lucky, she would never get her memory back and he would have a wife forever.

Sheriff Roscoe's nose twitched. Something did not smell right. So far, nothing sounded too off, but he knew to never discount his nose. "Why didn't you report her missin'?" As of that morning, there still was not any missing person in a three-state radius that could be even close to Claire. He had been checking every morning and night.

Scott sighed. He knew he would have to have a good story. And he did have a six-hour drive to come up with one. "We fought when we got home. I thought she just needed time to get over her anger and she'd come back. Yesterday, just before I saw her picture, I was preparing to report her missing."

"What'd ya fight 'bout?" The sheriff narrowed his eyes. He may still be single, but he did not know of any bride who fought on their wedding night. Unless the groom was a truly evil man. His instincts were telling him the man in question might be evil, and he did not seem like the type to catch a woman like Claire.

Plus, the name in Claire's dress. If her husband's name was not Brown, then hers would be. "What's Claire's maiden name?"

"Brown. Claire Brown."

Caleb and all his sons let out a breath. They knew the last name was not published anywhere. The sheriff had kept quiet about her being in a wedding dress with her name stitched into the tag. They wanted some way to keep anyone from finding out and possibly trying to trick them.

The sheriff crossed his arms over his chest. He still was not convinced this was Claire's husband. "Do you have your weddin' license?"

Scott blinked a few times and gave himself a moment to come up with a reply. "Not with me."

"I'll need a copy of it to make sure you and she were actually married."

"I... Well...I don't have it. The minister was going to file it with the county after the wedding." There, that should slow them down. With small-town bureaucracy, he had at least six months before anyone would expect him to have the filed and stamped license back.

The sheriff shook his head. "What about a copy? Surely you got a copy so Claire could change her driver's license."

"Actually, we didn't. The minister said it wouldn't take long to get the official one back, and with all the changes in laws lately, we decided to wait for the official copy so she could get one of them newfangled IDs. The kind that'll let her travel by plane out of state." He already had his Real ID and knew that copies of marriage licenses were not going to cut it when a bride wanted to change her name.

When he got his ID, he had to go the county recorder's office to get his original birth certificate. The faded copy he had in his safe at home would not suffice when he tried, so he knew a copy of a marriage license would not cut it, either.

'Uh, huh. And did you bring anything of hers with you? Like her purse or phone?" The sheriff was not about to give Claire to a man who had nothing more than a pretty story.

Scott sat back, deflated. "No, I was so worried about Claire that I didn't even think to bring her stuff."

"What about weddin' pictures?" Matthew asked. This was starting to look more and more like some sort of scam. Only Matthew did not know enough about Claire to understand why this man was trying to take a woman who was not his wife. She would get her memory back, and then he would be in a world of trouble if he was not actually her husband.

"They won't be ready for a while yet." Scott tried to look as though he was cooperating, but he was getting nervous. He had not expected to get the third degree. Maybe he should have taken another day and come up with proof?

John put his hand out. "Let me see your phone."

Scott's head jerked back. "Why?"

"Because I want to see the pictures of you and Claire, together." John glared at the man and knew he was lying. No man would marry a woman as beautiful as Claire and not have pictures of her on his phone.

"Well, I don't have any." Scott swallowed and felt a drop of sweat roll down the side of his face. He really should have thought this through better. Was it illegal to claim a woman with amnesia was his wife if she was not?

The sheriff put his hand on his revolver. "Stand up."

"What? Why?" The formerly cocky man was now sweating bullets and looked like a frightened rabbit.

Matthew smirked and knew Scott was most certainly *not* married to Claire.

Roscoe towered over the cowering man and pulled him up. "You're comin' with me."

Judith and Claire walked into the room with two trays of sweet tea.

Claire's eyes bulged when she saw the sheriff pulling Scott to his feet. "What's...happening?" To say she was shocked was an understatement. If that man was her husband, would he be so stupid to offend the sheriff enough to get arrested? It would be just her luck that she would have tied herself to an idiot.

"I'm taking Mr. Shelling here down to the station to get more detailed information from him." The sheriff had not handcuffed the man, but he sorely wanted to.

Mr. Manning took his wife's hand and stepped aside.

Matthew and Mark both stood guard next to Claire. They were not about to let anything happen to her. Especially not from some low-life, lying scumbag like Scott.

The sheriff stopped before he left the house and looked back over his shoulder. "If anyone else comes claimin' Miss Claire, be sure to send them my way and don't let them near the girl." He nodded and left.

"Of course, Sheriff." While John was the second-youngest and usually the quietest one of the group, he wasn't always like that.

He used to be more outgoing, and more inclined to get into a fight then any of the Manning boys. Since Claire arrived, he'd stepped up and started getting back some of his personality. In this case, he was acting like a big brother to Claire, even though she was most likely older than he was.

Caleb was proud of his sons for all sticking up for Claire. They had all been raised to treat women with respect and he knew that any one of his sons would take a bullet for a lady. And, one of his sons had already done so.

"So, does that mean that man isn't my husband?" Claire could not hold in the snort that came out of her mouth, and she bent over laughing. How in the world she could have thought he might have been her husband was beyond her.

"I wouldn't laugh too hard, yet." Mr. Manning stared at the door the sheriff left from and he hoped this little lady was not married to such a rotten excuse for a man. "While I doubt you would have married someone like that, it is still possible. He knew too much about you."

"I'm heading into town to see if I can find anything out about this Scott character." John scratched the stubble on his chin. "It is odd that he knew so much about our Claire."

Judith mouthed, *our Claire*? to her husband and raised her eyebrows. She thought she would have to worry about Matthew falling for the girl, not John. In fact, John had not even given a single woman a second look since he came home over a year ago.

With a hand over her mouth, Claire tried really hard to think about who she might have married. No headache came, and nothing flitted through her memory when she thought about Scott. The only feeling she had was one of revulsion. A chill skittered down her spine and she shook herself.

"Claire, are you alright?" Matthew had been silently watching the little filly, hoping to see if she would show any signs of familiarity for that man. But when she visibly shivered, he worried she may have been more affected by the situation than he realized.

She waved her hand. "No, I'm fine. It's just the thought of that man possibly being my husband disgusts me. If I really did marry him, please shoot me." She chuckled.

Mark pulled her into his arms. He patted her back like he

would have one of his sisters when they were upset. "There, there. I seriously doubt you were stupid enough to say 'I do' to that man."

The room broke out laughing, and Claire pulled back and punched Mark's shoulder, just like she was already part of this family.

"Alright, I think we've had enough excitement for one day." Judith looked at Claire. "Are you alright? Do you need a nap?"

Claire shook her head. "No, I'm fine...now. Can I help you prepare lunch?"

"That would be lovely, dear. Thank you." Judith smiled and took Claire's arm as they headed to the kitchen.

When the ladies were out of earshot, Caleb spoke up. "Sons, I need you all to be on the lookout for trouble. I doubt that's the only man who would have thought up such a scheme. We'll need to make sure that Claire doesn't go anywhere alone while she's here."

The boys all nodded.

"But what if he really is her husband?" Mark held up his hands.

All the Manning men began to disagree with him.

"Hear me out. I don't think she would have married such a person, but what if he had tricked her? And then the moment they were alone, she realized who he really was? That would be enough to make any sane woman flee. Don't you think?" Mark hoped that was not the case, but if that Scott was legally her husband, then they would have no choice but to surrender her to his care.

CHAPTER 17

"Dear Heavenly Father, thank you so much for keeping Claire safe, and for ensuring that rapscallion was discovered right away." Mr. Manning opened up their barbecue supper with gratefulness and a request for the truth to be known.

Claire did want the truth, but she also wanted this family. The entire Manning family was with her, save the daughter who moved away, and she felt like she belonged. Really and truly belonged here. She could not imagine being anywhere else. Even if Scott proved to be her husband, she still wanted to be here. Or maybe she wanted this life even more because of him?

"What's with that scowl?" Callie asked when she passed the potato salad to Claire.

"I'm sorry. An errant thought of him flew through my head." Claire served herself some of the creamy goodness and shook her head before passing the bowl to Matthew, who sat on her other side.

"That's not a headache forming, is it?" The last thing

Matthew wanted was for Claire to remember that Scott truly was her husband. He could deal with her being married, but not to *that* sorry excuse for a man.

Claire smiled and chuckled. "No, not a memory headache. More like a *I can't believe I would have been so silly to have married a man like him* type of ache."

At least she was able to joke about it. For now. Matthew hoped that when John returned, he would have some good news for them. He had been gone all afternoon, even missed lunch. Surely he'd have some news by now.

"Well, I say we plan to head out to Bozeman next weekend and you join us, Claire." Callie turned to Luke with a hopeful expression on her face.

Luke nodded and looked to Elizabeth, who was in charge of their excursions to help the homeless population of Bozeman. Their trip that day had been cancelled due to the unexpected arrival of Scott. Everyone said they supported staying in town to help Claire, and that they could all go the following weekend.

Elizabeth set her fork down on her plate and opened her mouth to respond. "I…"

"I have some news." A breathless John ran out to the back patio where the entire family was eating their Saturday evening barbecue steak dinner.

Everyone around the table hushed and looked expectantly at John.

Claire could not sit still. She was worried, but also hopeful. The expression on John's face was that of excitement. She doubted he would be excited to find out she was married to Scott. Well, unless he was ready for her and her drama to leave their peaceful ranch. Then maybe he would be happy.

"Scott's been arrested, and the feds were called in," John blurted out.

"What?" Claire and Matthew both declared together.

Judith clapped her hands, and Caleb raised a brow.

All of a sudden, everyone around the table began asking questions.

John put his hands up to quiet everyone and chuckled. "Give me a moment ta get the story out."

Once everyone quieted, John began to tell the story. "It seems Mr. Shelling came to town early this mornin' and hung out at the diner, listenin' to our own gossipmongers."

"So that's how he knew so much?" Elizabeth exclaimed. "I keep telling the Diner Divas they're going to cause someone to get hurt with their gossip. Maybe now they'll listen."

John gave his sister a pointed look, and she held up her hands.

"It seems Mr. Shelling is in desperate need of funds and figured Claire probably had a family with some money." John looked around at his family. "Or he thought we'd help them out. It seems he's heard about our charitable work."

"But..." Elizabeth put a hand over her mouth to keep quiet.

John nodded. "Yes. He thought he'd get himself a wife while also getting a handout from us."

"A wife he'd never in a million years get on his own." Mark snorted.

Claire shook her head. "But what if I got my memory back? I certainly wouldn't have stayed."

"I seriously doubt he thought that far in advance," John said as he walked to his spot at the table and sat down. "He didn't really plan this out very well. He saw a chance at a payday and a beautiful woman."

Claire's cheeks warmed, and she looked down at her plate.

"Hey, don't worry. We'll find your family." Callie put a hand on Claire's and squeezed.

"And until such time as we find your other family, you can call us family." Mr. Manning smiled at his newly adopted daughter and decided no matter what, they were going to take care of Claire.

A warmth spread through Claire, and she gave Mr. Manning her best smile.

Matthew had to look away from the angelic look on Claire's face. Today's debacle only enforced the fact that Claire was off-limits. While she was not married to that fool, she could very well be married to someone out there. The only thing he could not understand was why no one was looking for her. What sort of family would let a woman like Claire disappear and not try to find her?

An uncomfortable feeling began to creep in, and he wondered if maybe she had escaped something truly horrific, and her family could not be looking for her. But wouldn't they have heard if something that awful happened? Even if it was halfway across the country?

LATER THAT NIGHT, Matthew sat in front of his computer and looked up any and all weddings reported on in the last week. Then he looked for news about a wedding massacre. Thankfully, there were no reported situations. He knew the news well enough to know that if something like that did happen, it would have been reported all over the internet.

He conducted a search for Claire Brown. Even removing the references to fictional doctors, there were almost four hundred thousand entries. He leaned back and sighed. "No wonder the sheriff hasn't found anything yet. It would take an entire school of social media experts looking for a year to sort through all of these entries."

Matthew was not pleased with his lack of information. Without knowing exactly who she was, the poor filly was stuck. Not that he minded her being with his family. In fact, he had never been happier that he was the one who found her. But he could not imagine what it would be like to try and remember something as simple as his last name, or his family.

If he were to ever forget the ranch, he would be heartbroken. This place was the only home he had ever known, or ever would know. He could not even remember a time when he wanted to leave the Triple J. Some of his ranch friends had dreamt about leaving town when they were kids, but those who did leave almost always came home. Sure, there were a few kids from school who moved away, never to return outside of Christmas, but those were the exceptions.

Family was an integral part of the ranch life. Not just because ranchers needed the extra hands to make a go of it, but because it flowed through their blood, literally. Families who lived together, worked together, and played together were strong and loving. They did not want anything else.

Then there were those who had been here working the land for generations. Matthew was convinced this life had permeated the DNA of those who operated generational ranches and farms.

Ranching was in his genes, and he would never forget it.

That's when it hit him. "Ranching and farming is in our genes. The way Claire took to horses was natural, not learned."

He refined his search and began looking for beauty contestants from rodeos in the area who might have matched

Claire's looks and age. He guessed she was about twenty-eight or so. He doubted she was thirty.

Then, when he found too many entries, he refined his search to just certain years.

CHAPTER 18

A loud knock caused Matthew to jump, and a moan escaped his mouth. He rubbed the ache in his neck and looked down. He had fallen asleep at the small desk in his room.

"Matthew, you're gonna be late."

Mark's voice got his attention and he looked at the clock. "Blast it all." He jumped up and ran a hand through his hair. "Mark, I'll drive myself to church." He could not believe he'd fallen asleep at his computer and now was going to be late for church. Matthew hated being late for anything, especially church.

"Alright, but you better hurry. Pa's gonna say something to the Diner Divas about their gossiping and how they almost caused an innocent woman to be kidnapped by an outlaw." Mark walked away and headed to the kitchen, where he put on a fresh pot of coffee for his eldest brother.

If Matthew had slept in so long, that meant he was either sick or had been up all night. Either way, he would need coffee to get going.

Judith watched her middle child set up the coffee for

Matthew, and she pulled out some jerky and a granola bar to add to the offering. "Come on, let's get going. We don't want the entire family to be late, do we?"

Mark grinned and followed his mother out to the truck.

Caleb Manning had arrived at church early with a mission. His younger son, John, was with him. Mark and Luke were not too far behind with their mother and Claire. Caleb wanted to say his piece before Claire arrived and became embarrassed.

The town gossips had been allowed too much leeway, and it was time someone stopped them. He could not imagine what would have happened to Claire if Scott had absconded with the sweet young lady under his roof.

It was a good thing his future daughter-in-law was a sheriff's deputy. Her visit last night had stopped him from heading down to the sheriff's station and giving the criminal a what for. Callie calmly informed him that should he attempt to hurt a prisoner in their possession, the sheriff would have to arrest him.

Caleb was not worried about getting arrested, at least not for himself. But he was worried about what might happen to his wife and Claire if they were left without him to protect them. Sure, his sons would step up and do a good job, but a cowboy never let someone else take care of the women under his charge if he could help it.

Then his wife reminded him of his witness. Should he be arrested for assault, no matter how much the crook deserved it, it would hurt his witness and he would most likely lose his position as a church deacon. Hot heads were not good role models.

While he was still angry, he had let most of it go before he went to bed. He had spent at least an hour on his knees praying to the good Lord and asking for peace as well as forgiveness for his anger.

But this was something he felt led to do.

When Caleb saw the leader of the divas, he stalked her way.

Cindy Macon looked his way with a huge smile, and he wondered how she could be so happy after what she did.

He did notice that her smile quickly left her face and was soon replaced with shame. As it should be. Her eyes were downcast, and she began to fiddle with the handle on her purse.

"Mr. Manning. Good morning." Cindy still could not look him in the eyes.

She knew what she had done.

"Well, what do you have to say for yourself?" Caleb fisted his hands at his sides, but stayed far enough away from the bothersome woman to keep the wagging tongues at bay.

"I'm sorry." Cindy wrung her hands and looked around for help. She knew Caleb Manning would never hurt her, but the anger she saw on his face had her doubting what she knew about him.

John stood behind his father and shook his head. He was very disappointed in the woman who at one time had taught his Sunday school class. As a child, she had seemed like a paragon of virtue and uprightness. Now, he wondered what had happened to her.

"Sorry—is that all you have to say?" John asked when his father stayed quiet a few ticks too long.

"No, but I think I need to speak with Claire first." Cindy sighed and looked past the two Manning men.

"She's comin, but I wanted to speak with you first." Caleb was a tall man, and at that moment he towered over Cindy as though she was nothing more than a child. "Thanks to you and your crew of waggin' tongues, a young, innocent woman was almost abducted from my ranch."

"I know. The sheriff spoke with me just this morning. And I feel awful. Truly, I do." The pleading in her eyes was not a lie. She did want his forgiveness, as well as Claire's.

"And what do you plan to do in order to make amends?" Caleb had to stop himself from snarling and hoped that the menace in his voice was enough to get Cindy back on track.

"I… Well, I think it's time we take our seats." She looked to the minister, who walked toward them.

"Caleb." Pastor Baker smiled at his deacon and turned to look at Cindy. "I'm getting ready to start services now. Please take your seats."

"Of course, Pastor," Caleb grumbled, and did as his pastor said. He and John went to their family pew and sat down. Not long after, the rest of his family—minus Matthew—took their seats and the piano began to play the opening hymn.

MATTHEW HATED that he was so late. Not only was he exhausted, but he was no closer to finding out who Claire really was. Thankfully, his family had taken care of him and he was now on the way into town with a thermos full of hot, black coffee and a few pieces of jerky, and a granola bar. While it was not the best breakfast, it would get him through services.

Sunday afternoons they always had a large spread for lunch, and he was certain he would be able to get a snack to tide him over until it was all ready. Now, he needed to keep his eyes on the road and get to church before the sermon began.

Which was exactly what he did. Not wanting to disturb the congregation, he took a seat in the back of the church right before the pastor read from the Bible. He had been doing a lot of sermons on forgiveness lately, and Matthew figured it would be a similar sermon that day.

He could not have been more wrong. The pastor opened the message up with a verse from 1 Timothy chapter 5, verse 13 – *And withal they learn to be idle, wandering about from house to house; and not only idle, but tattlers also and busybodies, speaking things which they ought not.*

The pastor looked at the congregation. "The context is in regards to widows and what happens when women who don't have enough work to do begin to spread gossip." He was careful to look at everyone, not just the Diner Divas. They were not the only ones who gossiped. They just happened to be the group who did it the most.

Matthew looked around for Cindy and her crew and noticed they were squirming in their seats. The verse was spot on. All four of them were older women who no longer had families to take care of. Not all were widowed, but none had children or jobs to keep them busy.

He wondered how this sermon was going to go down. Would others realize they were also guilty of telling tall tales? Being tattlers and busybodies? Always having to know what their neighbors were up to and sharing their stories about town?

Matthew did not think anyone in town was completely innocent. Even he had spread gossip a time or two. But he did not think he'd done it with malicious intent, and neither had the divas. But what they spread did cause the situation to be worse than it could have been.

The pastor continued to talk about wisdom and holding one's tongue. Matthew was surprised by all the references in the Bible to gossip and how it brought people down the path to destruction.

If he had not known how dangerous gossip was before the situation the day before, he certainly did now. No matter what, Scott would have shown up, but he would not have been allowed to stay so long had he not known so much about Claire. Every minute that man was in his home, Claire hurt more and more.

Shoot, *he* hurt more and more with every story that came from the man's lips. Lies and deceit were also included in the admonitions of the Bible. Gossip was listed along with lies.

When the pastor read Proverbs 18:8, Matthew felt the pain Claire must have endured and probably still did. *The words of a talebearer are as wounds, and they go down into the innermost parts of the belly.*

He looked at Claire, but since she was so far in front of him, he could not see her face well enough to know what she was feeling. He could only guess as to what might have been going through her mind and heart.

When the service was over, all four Diner Divas made their way to the Manning family pews.

Matthew hurried over to ensure they were not going to say or do anything to cause Claire even more harm.

He was surprised to see Claire hug Cindy and her crew.

"I know you didn't intend any harm. And I forgive you." Claire's small smile did not reach her eyes, but it was genuine.

"Claire"—Matthew put a hand to her elbow—"are you alright?"

She turned to see him, and her smiled widened. "Yes, thank you."

He turned his gaze on the elderly women in front of him and was not sure what to say. If Claire forgave them, who was he to hold a grudge?

It seemed the pastor's sermons on forgiveness were

directed by God in anticipation of the events unfolding all around Matthew. A year ago, he may not have forgiven so easily. But he knew he had to. God commanded we forgive those who hurt us seven times seventy times.

Caleb grumbled, but knew he had to let it go fully and do exactly what Claire had done—forgive the women. It seemed God wasn't done teaching him lessons, or dealing with him and his anger.

The pastor came over and smiled at the group. "I see friendships are being mended."

Judith smiled at the leader of their church. "Yes, Pastor. And I think we all need to think more about how to help those in our own community who might need something to do. Idleness is the hands of the enemy."

Pastor Baker chuckled and said as he left, "That it is, that it is."

Elizabeth put a finger to her chin. "I think you ladies should join us next weekend when we head out to Bozeman."

Lou Ann Dobbs' eyebrows rose, and she gasped. "But, I've heard about that Bart fellow. Will it be safe for us?"

Mark nodded. "Yes, Mrs. Dobbs. I'll be right beside you and protect you should there be a need."

Elizabeth chuckled. "We don't allow anyone to work alone, and all women must have at least one man in their party, for protection."

"Isn't that a bit sexist?" Claire asked with furrowed brows.

Everyone looked to Elizabeth and waited for her to answer. It was her rule, after all.

With a huge smile, Elizabeth answered, "Well, when we first started out, it was me and a group of ladies. We were able to defend ourselves when Bart tried to attack us, but when we returned with men, Bart and his gang weren't as…"

She looked around, trying to find the right word. "Let's just say that having men with us, even though we could all take care of ourselves, helped to keep the bad guys at bay."

Logan wrapped his arms around his wife. "And I for one feel much better knowing that I'm close by when Elizabeth does have to interact with Bart or any of his crew."

Elizabeth slapped his hands. "Hey, you know I can take care of myself." She arched a brow.

The lazy smile that crossed Logan's face told Elizabeth he did know. "Yes, but I am a caveman, after all."

All the women laughed, and Logan leaned down and kissed his wife on the cheek.

Tears pricked the backs of Claire's eyes. She prayed her husband loved her as much as Logan obviously loved his wife.

CHAPTER 19

"How have you felt since you left here?" Doc Montgomery shone the flashlight pen in Claire's eyes.

"I'm much better than when I first left." She saw bright light and spots when he moved the light out of her face.

The doctor stood and put a few notes in the file. "What about the headaches?"

"I take it Harper told you about them?" Every day Harper had been over for dinner and asked Claire about her headaches, and memory. For the past three days the only times she had a headache were when she tried to force a memory out. Otherwise, no headaches.

He nodded.

"I'm actually surprised at how good I feel. Even the body aches are almost gone." She had taken long, hot showers each night and let the water pound her aching muscles. "And thanks to the mother hen, I've been taking Advil on a regular basis." Claire giggled.

Doc Montgomery snorted. "Yeah, Judith can be a little bit of a mother hen. She's been a great nurse to you?"

"Judith?" Claire scrunched her forehead and then

laughed. "I meant Matthew. He's been asking me every six hours or so if I've taken my meds."

They both laughed.

"But, Judith has been great as well. She's not pushed me to do anything. In fact, she tries to get me to sleep a lot." Claire frowned. "Too much, actually."

"Hmm." The doctor nodded and wrote some more notes. "Now tell me about any memories you've had."

Claire did not have anything to tell him. All she'd had were foggy, or ghostlike, wisps of outlines. Nothing really concrete that she could grab onto. "The only thing I really feel like I know for sure is that I love horses. And..." She bit her lip, not sure how to explain what she felt. "I don't think I'm married."

The doctor took a seat across from her and put his pen and file down. "Tell me more about that. How do you know you aren't?"

She took a deep breath and let it out slowly. "I take it you've heard about the man who came out claiming to be my husband?"

He nodded.

"Well, when I first saw him it didn't feel right." She paused.

"But don't you think that might have been because he wasn't your husband? He was a fake," the doctor supplied.

Claire nodded. "Possibly. But I've thought more about it since Saturday and I just don't have peace about being married." She held up her hands. "I know, I was in a wedding dress. But think about it. I didn't have a wedding ring on, not even an engagement ring."

"But don't you think you might have lost it in your accident?" Doc Montgomery leaned forward and looked at Claire's hand. There was a small tan mark where a ring would have been if she was engaged or married and wore the ring for a while.

Claire noticed where the doctor was looking, and she saw the mark as well. "I do think I was probably engaged. That line confirms that I did wear a ring for a while. At least long enough to make a tan line."

He nodded. "Okay, then why do you think you aren't actually married?"

"Because it doesn't feel right." She shook her head. "I know, it sounds strange. But when I've tried to picture my husband and force a memory, nothing comes."

"Can you force a memory for something else?" he asked.

She nodded. "Well, not a full memory. But when I concentrate and try to think about my horse, I get a headache and an outline appears only to just disappear into the ether." Claire shrugged. "Other images and feelings have been similar. When I focus and try to remember, a headache develops and I get glimpses. Nothing that really makes any sense, but enough that I know those are real. However, when I try to remember my husband, nothing."

She really did want to remember her life, and if she was even married.

"It makes me think that something might have happened to me on the way to the church. I wouldn't have had on any rings if I was on my way to getting married. But I would have worn my dress to the church if it was a small church, right?" Even movies showed brides riding to the church in their dress, when it was a small wedding. Only those large, fancy weddings had rooms where the bride would change once she was at the church.

Just the night before she watched one with Judith, Elizabeth, and Callie. Once the movie was over, all the women looked at her expectantly, hoping she'd remember something.

It was not until after the movie that she realized why they had chosen that one.

At first, she just thought they had weddings on the brain since Elizabeth was newly wed and Callie would be getting engaged to Luke very soon.

But nothing triggered a memory. She did wonder about that. Even if she was on her way to her wedding, wouldn't she remember something? When she went to bed, she started to think that maybe she was not even engaged. Maybe she worked at a dress shop and fell in love with that dress she had on. Although, why would she have her name sewn into it if that was the case?

The last name of Brown never felt right, either. It was most likely her fiancé's last name. She was just as confused as when she first woke up. It took her a while to fall asleep, and when she did, all she dreamed about was Matthew riding a white horse and taking her away from her troubles.

She really needed to stop watching those romance movies with the ladies of the Triple J.

With pen in hand, the doctor began writing notes again. When he finished, he looked up at his patient. "Tell me about where you grew up."

Claire thought about home and all she could see was the Triple J Ranch. "I can't."

"Think harder."

She sighed and closed her eyes. A scent enveloped her. "Night Jasmine? Roses? Maybe lavender? I think…" She winced and put a hand to her temple and rubbed. "I think I have a flower garden, but I can't seem to get it." She moaned and put her other hand to her other temple. "Oh." She sighed and stopped herself from looking any further.

"Don't worry. I don't want to cause any pain." He sighed and sat back in his chair. "I don't want you to try and force any more memories for now. If they come, let them come on their own."

"Why do you think I can't remember anything?" Claire continued to rub her temples and kept her eyes closed.

"I think there's more going on than physical trauma. I think something happened that's keeping you from remembering. Our subconscious knows when to protect us." The doctor scratched his forehead and considered the case in front of him. "It's possible your mind doesn't want you to remember, and that's why you keep getting headaches when you try to force it."

Claire nodded. "But that doesn't explain why no one is looking for me. You'd think that if I was engaged, my fiancé at the very least would have begun looking for me by now. Wouldn't he?" She bit her lip, hoping that someone was looking for her.

"There could be a million reasons why your family isn't looking for you yet. I think for now, you need to focus on the here and how. Just do chores around the ranch, take daily rides. Do what feels right to you. Getting into a familiar routine could do wonders for your memory." The doctor stood up and motioned for Claire to follow him.

"So, that's it? Have fun?" The incredulous look on her face caused the doctor to smile.

"Sometimes it's the simple things in life that do the most healing."

Matthew had been in the waiting room during Claire's appointment. His mother had wanted someone else to take her into town, but he was not about to let her out of his sight if she was in town. Who knew how many more psychos were out there thinking they could claim her as their own?

He tried sitting and reading a magazine, but found he was

too wound up to stay still. So when Claire came out of the exam room, he was pacing the short length of the room.

"Claire, so what'd the doc say?" Matthew did not realize how nervous he was for her response. It was too soon for there to be any big news, but he did hope that she was doing at least as well as could be expected.

"He said to get into a routine and have fun." She shrugged.

"Well, it's a bit more than that." Doc Montgomery chuckled and reached a hand out to Matthew. "Good to see you again, Matthew."

He shook the doctor's hand and replied, "You, too." Matthew looked between the doctor and Claire, waiting for someone to tell him what was going on.

"I want to see you back here again in two weeks. Keep taking the Advil as long as you feel aches and pains." The doctor turned toward Matthew. "I think she can start doing as much as she wants, just as long as she doesn't overdo it. I want to see her get into the routine of a rancher. Maybe even do some gardening if possible."

"Of course, Doc. I'm sure Ma will have her workin' in the garden by tomorrow." Matthew's mom did have a flower garden, but they also grew some of their own vegetables and fruits, along with spices.

"Great, but this afternoon I want to go on a long ride," Claire squeaked, and practically jumped in place.

Matthew raised a brow and looked to the doctor.

Doc Montgomery chuckled. "Yes, you can ride as much as you feel you can handle. Just don't overdo it. I don't need you back in here because you've fainted from exhaustion. Be sure to keep eating healthy, and drink lots of water."

"Thank you, Doctor. We'll take good care of her." Matthew put his hat on and walked Claire to his truck.

"Well, it seems that went well. What did he say about your memory?" Matthew opened the passenger door for Claire and helped her in before closing the door.

When he got in on the driver's side, he looked to Claire for her response.

"He thinks my subconscious is blocking me from remembering." She bit the inside of her cheek and thought about it for a minute.

Matthew took in what she had said and wondered what could have happened to cause her to forget, and her mind to keep her from remembering. It had to have been extremely traumatic.

"What do you think?" Before he said anything about his thoughts, he needed to know what she was thinking.

She shrugged. "I'm not really sure. I mean, it makes sense. But if something bad happened at the wedding, wouldn't the sheriff have found out by now?"

"Hmm, why don't we pay him a visit and see if he has any more leads?" Matthew turned the truck on and backed out of the parking spot.

When they were just down the street from the station, Claire put a hand on his arm. "Wait. Will we see that creep, Scott?" She trembled when she thought about him and what he almost got away with.

Matthew slowed and thought about it. "I don't think so. I can call the sheriff first if you want. The feds were supposed to take him in yesterday."

"Okay, then let's go." She was going to be strong and not worry. The feds had the stalker and even if they had not left yet, he was behind bars. She doubted she'd even see the jail cells. It wasn't like this was Mayberry and the cell was in a one-roomed sheriff's office. And the sheriff certainly was not a Barney Fife type of character. She would be just fine.

CHAPTER 20

It may not have been a one-roomed office, but it sure was close to it.

Only a door separated the jail cells from the open area where the sheriff and his deputies had desks.

"Claire, Matthew. What can I do for you?" The sheriff smiled and put the notepad he was reading down on his desk.

Claire licked her lips. "We've come by to see if you've heard anything new?" Her hopeful voice raised on the word *new*.

Roscoe put his hands on his utility belt and stood. "I'm sorry, but nothin' new yet. I haven't given up. And you shouldn't, either."

When a hand grazed her lower back, Claire jumped.

"Sorry, I was just tryin' to comfort you." Matthew kicked himself mentally for touching her, especially at that moment. It was just that he felt the need to connect to her, and that she might need human contact.

The pain he saw in her eyes when the sheriff told her there was not any news almost broke his heart for her. If she had been his wife, fiancé, or even girlfriend, he would not have let her disappear. He would have moved heaven and earth to find her. And he most certainly would have filed a missing person's report.

A thought hit him. "Sheriff, we've been assumin' she's from here. What if she's from Canada?" While they were in southern Montana, Canada was their neighbor to the north. It was very possible she had come from there. If so, it would explain why they hadn't any luck yet with finding her family.

Light entered her eyes, and she looked to the sheriff expectantly.

The sheriff rubbed his chin and nodded. "I s'pose that's possible. I'll have to reach out the to the State Department to get them to look into it. It could take several days before we hear anything, but it's worth it." He nodded and yelled for Callie to join them.

Callie had been on the other side of the room trying to get some studying done since she had a test later that week. It would be her final test and then she would be a full-fledged deputy.

"Yes, Sheriff?" She had heard what they were discussing. Even though she tried not to listen, the room was too small for any private conversations to be had. But, she'd try to act as though she hadn't been paying attention.

'Why don't you get a ten-card from Claire here and upload it to the system so I can get the boys over at State to contact the Mounties?"

"Ten-card?" Claire asked. When she looked at Matthew and saw he was just as confused as she was, she realized it probably was not something she had ever known and just forgotten. It did not sound like something laypeople would know.

"Care to explain it to the little lady?" the sheriff asked Callie.

The young deputy-in-training smiled and motioned for Claire to follow her to the side of the room where her desk was located. "It's your fingerprints. We used to put them on cards and since you have ten fingers, it was called a ten-card."

"But you don't put them on cards anymore?" Matthew asked.

Callie laughed. "Actually, we do. Then we scan them into the system. But, most big cities have the digital technology to just scan your prints. We don't have the budget to upgrade."

"The joys of small-town livin'." Matthew chuckled.

After Callie had taken Claire's prints, she handed the young woman a wet nap and went to work on scanning the prints into their system to be sent to the State Department.

"Why did you need my prints to ask Canada about me?" Claire threw the dirty wet nap into the bin next to Callie's desk and waited for the woman to respond.

"We'll have to send your picture, prints, and a physical description of you to the Mounties. They'll want to look at all avenues before they'll know if you're one of theirs or not." Callie winced. "But, you should know they're slower than molasses on a cold winter's night."

Claire could not help it, she laughed. One thing she did not lack was things to make her laugh around here. "I'm not worried. I understand that I have to wait a while to hear back. While I don't feel peace about this, it is something that's being done other than waiting around for a report to be filed on me."

At least with the possibility that she was from Canada, she felt better about not having family looking for her. It actually made sense.

"You know, if you were a kid we'd have gotten word about you missing within hours of the Mounties taking the report. But for adults, it's a totally different process." Callie shook her head. When she first learned how the Amber Alerts were sent, and who could send them, she asked about adults. Sadly, only missing children were reported using this international tool.

"It's a great tool, but I think it might help locate adults as well. Think of all the women who've been kidnapped and sold into slavery who might be saved." Callie shook her head. "Sorry, it's one the issues I'd like to take up one day should I ever become sheriff."

"I heard that," Sheriff Roscoe yelled. "And I'll fully support you."

"Then maybe you can support me now?" Callie yelled back.

He grumbled something, but no one could make it out.

"Why doesn't he work on that now?" Claire asked.

"It's a political issue." Callie sighed. She hated politics, which was why she would probably never run for sheriff.

"No, it's a manpower issue. Politics have nothing to do with women goin' missin'." The sheriff shook his head. "Are you finished with her prints?"

"Yes, sir. I've already scanned them. They're ready for you to add to the file when you send it." Callie walked Claire and Matthew to the front door. "I'll see you both later. I think Luke's having me out for dinner later this week."

"Perfect. And thank you." Claire took the deputy's hand and squeezed it before exiting the building.

Claire did not talk much on the way home. Instead, she tried to think about who her family might be, and where in Canada she could be from. Before they made the final turn into the lane that led up to the ranch, she turned in her seat to look at Matthew.

"How could I know geography so well, but not my own last name?" On the way home she had been thinking about the fifty American states, and then the ten Canadian provinces. She had a clear picture in her mind of both countries. But she had no clue where on either map she could pin her home.

She could, however, stick a pin in the spot on the Montana map where the Triple J was located.

"Do you think you know Canada well?" He was not sure if it was important or meant anything, but if she knew Canada better than the US, she might be a Canuck.

Her gaze roamed the dusty drive as they drove up the front of the ranch. "I don't know which I know better. Maybe after supper we can look up maps and I can get a better feel for both countries?"

He nodded. "That sounds like a great idea. But first, how 'bout a ride?"

Matthew turned his thousand-watt smile on her, and she almost melted under his hazel-eyed stare. She noted flecks of gold that glittered when the sun hit his eyes just right.

When she bounced in her seat, they both laughed, and he turned his gaze back out the front window.

"I'll take that as a yes." He stopped the truck out front of the house and got out, then went around to help Claire out.

The moment Claire sat in the saddle, she sighed. "This is perfection. I'd be more than happy to spend the rest of my life in a saddle."

After he swung his leg over Thunder and put both boots in the stirrups and looked at Claire for just a moment, he could have sworn he saw an image of them both riding together thirty years down the road.

He shook his head and led them out of the paddock and into the fields.

"So, has the neighbor's bull been visiting his sweethearts lately?" Claire laughed and looked to Matthew.

He snorted and urged Thunder on faster. "He keeps tryin', and we keep reinforcin' the fence lines."

"Awww, you should let him in. He's missin' his ladies. That's mean to keep them apart." She urged Whiskers on and pulled up next to Matthew as they galloped closer to the fence lines.

"Really? You think I should let a horny ol' bull in to spend time with our cows? How do you think they feel about it?" He doubted they minded. Several of his cows usually stayed closer to the Johnson fence lines than the others, so they probably enjoyed the bull's company.

"Put yourself in his shoes. How would you feel if some ornery rancher kept you away from the woman you loved?"

"It might actually be better than being this close and not allowed to touch her," He whispered and hoped she did not pick it up.

She looked over at him quickly and furrowed her brows. "What was that?"

"I'd fight for any woman I wanted." Well, as long as she was single. He was not about to fight for a married woman, no matter how much he wanted to.

"Then let's open the gate and let that ol' bull have some fun." She clicked her tongue and kicked Whiskers' flanks.

Matthew grinned and followed her lead.

Sure enough, as soon as they got near the Johnson fence line the ol' bull was sniffin' 'round to find a weakness.

Matthew laughed at the bull's antics and looked around to see which parts of their stock were nearby. There were some younger heifers who were not quite yet ready to breed. He would have to make sure they were in a different pasture if he was going to let the bull in.

He would prefer it if only a few of the older cows that the bull seemed to be sweet on were nearby. But first, he would have to ask Mr. Johnson if he minded him letting the bull on their side of the fence. Maybe he could arrange a date of sorts for the mean ol' bull later in the week, after they moved the cattle around.

From past experiences, the bull was very territorial and would go after any male steers they had nearby before claiming his prizes. It seemed the ol' bull didn't like competition, even if the male steer in the field didn't have the same equipment a bull did.

"So, whatcha gonna do?" The teasing lilt in Claire's voice caught Matthew's attention.

He grinned. "I'll tell ya what I'm gonna do." He drew closer to the little filly and when he was up right next to Whiskers, he slapped her hind quarter and watched as the horse took off at a gallop with Claire screaming in pure pleasure.

"Yee haw!" Claire's smile spread from one side of her face to the other as she raced away from the Johnson fence line and farther into the Manning fields. She kicked Whiskers' sides to get more speed after she looked over her shoulder.

Right on her tail was Thunder and his rider. She knew she would lose in a fair race, hands down. But he was the one that forced a head start on her. She was not going to let it go to waste.

With her braid flying behind her and the wind whipping through her bangs, she let herself feel everything around her. The tension she had built up from the day's events slid off her like water on oil.

Without a care in the world, she smiled at the sky in front of her and enjoyed the exhilarating ride on Whiskers. "Come on, girl. Don't let that fussy pants beat you. You got this." She urged her horse on, and it was as though Whiskers understood what she was saying; the horse sped up just enough to keep Thunder and Matthew on their tail.

"H'ya!" Matthew said, and urged Thunder to go faster. He could not believe that Claire and Whiskers were still ahead of him. "Come on, boy. Do you really want a *girl* to beat you?" The horse increased his speed just enough to get his head past Whiskers' tail, but he was not going to overtake the other horse—not in time to win.

The other fence was coming up quick.

"Whoever gets to the oak tree first wins," Matthew yelled out as he urged his horse to go faster.

Claire did not look over her shoulder; not only was it too dangerous, but she knew where the cowboy was based on the sound of the other horse's hooves and Matthew's voice. He was close. Too close.

"Come on, Whiskers, you got this," she encouraged her horse.

Out of the corner of her eye, Claire saw Thunder's nose inching closer and closer. If Whiskers did not pick up her pace, she'd lose. No way did she want to lose her first horse race that she could remember.

Claire kicked Whiskers again. Not too hard—not hard enough to hurt the horse, but enough to get her intentions through. "Don't let a boy beat you."

Again it was as though Whiskers understood the importance of this race, and she heaved harder and pushed forward just enough to claim victory.

Matthew could not believe it. He had never lost to a mare before. And certainly not to Whiskers. That horse had never run so fast in her life. It was almost as though a rattler were on her tail and she was running for her life.

When she beat him by a nose, he pulled back on his reins. "Whoa, whoa, Thunder." As they slowed down, he ran a hand down his horse's neck and let him know he did good. Even though he wanted to ask why he let a girl beat him, the horse still did good.

Maybe Thunder knew how important it was for Whiskers to win a race? He was not sure.

Spring was in the air, so maybe Thunder had a thing for the pretty mare? There was definitely a lot of *that* going around lately.

"Good race," Claire said when she turned around and stopped next to Thunder and Matthew.

"You mean great race, don't you?" he responded.

Had it been anyone other than Claire on Whiskers, he would have been put out losing to them, but for some reason he did not mind losing to Claire.

She beamed at him.

"You've got a great seat. I'd bet you're an experienced rider, and racer." He eyed her with a different thought in mind. She still did not look familiar, but he wondered if she was a horse trainer.

The way she pulled the speed out of Whiskers was unreal. Not only did she have a natural ability with the horses, she also had skill. And she sat so regally upon the horse, something most experienced riders had trouble doing. But she did it naturally.

"Huh, I suppose it's possible. I did love it." She grinned and clicked her tongue. Whiskers moved without much effort from Claire.

If Matthew did not know better, he'd say the horse was proud of beating them and held her head just a bit higher. Her tail swooshed right into Thunder's face when they passed him, and Matthew chuckled. "It seems we have a cheeky rider for a cheeky horse."

"If the horseshoe fits…" The little filly and her mare trotted away chuckling.

CHAPTER 21

They did not go back right away. Instead, they continued checking the fence lines and just enjoying the clean air and warm sun shining down on them as they rode and chatted about everything and nothing. It was not as though Claire had many stories to share, so they talked about horses and ranching, mostly.

By the time they made it home, Matthew knew something was wrong.

He knew they were late for supper, but it did not necessitate the sheriff waiting for them in the paddock along with Matthew's pops.

Matthew looked to Claire and saw the moment she realized something was off. Her smile quickly changed to a frown and she looked at Matthew.

"What's wrong? It's too soon for them to have heard back from Canada, isn't it?" Claire asked.

Without knowing what it could be, he could not exactly answer her questions. Instead, he guided them toward the growing group of family members near the paddock.

When he and Claire were only a few paces from the sheriff, they stopped and dismounted. While he knew Claire was skilled enough to get herself down from a horse, he still wished she would have waited for him to help her. It would probably have been his last opportunity to do so, and he wanted to remember how she felt in his arms.

The sheriff stood in front of Matthew with a smile a mile long. The only thing it could mean was that the sheriff had found her family. Why else would he be waiting for them and looking so happy? His mother, however, did not look so happy. She looked at him with worry covering her face.

His mother knew how he felt about Claire—she had even warned him this day would come. Told him she was most likely married, and he had no business getting close to her. Matthew had tried to keep a respectful distance, but the little filly was so easy to relax with.

The past week had been perfection. Well, except the part about Scott. But every moment he had spent with her he'd cherish and keep close to his heart. Matthew was not sure if it was better she was leaving so soon, or if he wanted more time with her. Time to make more memories for when she was gone, living with another man. Would she treasure this time they had together? Or would she shelve the memories away as an adventure she had once had?

"Sheriff, do you have news?" Matthew had to be strong. He looked at the faces of his family and saw the pain in their eyes. Pain they felt for him. He knew it.

"What do you say we all go inside and have some sweet tea?" Judith offered.

"Does this mean you found something?" Claire wrung her hands, and part of her heart broke as the other part jumped in anticipation of learning who she was.

If she found her family, that would mean she would have to leave the Triple J, and Matthew. Claire was not sure she was ready to leave him yet. She certainly was not ready to leave his ranch and Whiskers. Somehow in the past few days she had bonded with the horse, and the land.

Sheriff Roscoe tipped his hat in Claire's direction. "Ma'am, after you left today I received a call from a sheriff in Red Creek. He saw your picture on social media."

Claire gulped. This was it. She was going to discover who she was, and if she was married.

Matthew opened the door for everyone and stood to the side, holding it as his family and the sheriff entered.

When Claire walked past him, she could not bring herself to look him in the eyes. Instead, she whispered, "Thank you."

She was not sure why she was not more excited to find out her true identity, but she was not. Not if it meant leaving Beacon Creek and the Mannings.

Judith led the way to the living room and motioned for everyone to sit. When she turned to leave the room for refreshments, Claire moved to follow her.

"No dear, stay here and find out what news the sheriff has. I'll be fine getting the drinks myself." Judith patted Claire's arm.

John followed his mother into the kitchen to help instead of taking a seat with everyone else.

Claire slowly walked to a seat next to Matthew on the sofa and sat down.

When the sheriff took a seat in an easy chair across from her, the rest of the room sat down and waited.

"There is a family who reported you missing only today." The sheriff took in the solemn looks around him and frowned. "They emailed me a copy of your passport and driver's license. Your name is Claire Stapleton and you were supposed to marry Brad Brown the day you disappeared."

"Supposed to?" Claire latched onto the choice of words and wondered if she was still single.

Matthew took her hand in his, and his heart beat fast as they waited for the sheriff to respond.

Roscoe noted the way Matthew held Claire's hand and lifted a brow. "Yes, you ran before the ceremony started."

"Then where's her car? Or did she hitchhike?" Caleb Manning asked.

The sheriff cleared his throat and was about to start when Judith and John walked in with trays of iced tea.

As soon as everyone had a drink and the two had seated themselves, the sheriff continued. "It seems you took off on your horse and bolted. When your horse finally showed up at home earlier today, your family knew something was really wrong and called the local sheriff."

"My horse? Why did they wait until my horse came back without me?" Now Claire was confused. Did she normally run? Was she like those runaway brides in the movies? Surely this was not her normal move, was it?

The sheriff coughed and took another sip of his tea before setting it down. He picked up his hat and turned it around in his hands. "Well, it seems you and your fiancé had a fight and you ran away before anything could be discussed. When your folks found out why you ran, they decided to give you some space and wait for you to return."

"Her parents let her leave without a purse, phone, or even money and didn't think she needed their help? What kind of parents would do that?" Caleb would never have let any of his kids run away without him checking on them.

"They thought she'd ended up at a friend's house and didn't want to talk to anyone. Since she did not have money, clothes, or a phone, they expected she went into hiding with a friend. They were about to call the sheriff when the horse came into the yard." Roscoe stood and went to a window to look out the back of the house.

"They will be here tomorrow mornin' to see ya."

"So, I'm not married?" Claire had to be sure she understood her situation.

Nothing had triggered a memory yet, and she had no idea who Brad was, or who her parents were. The only thing she needed at that moment was to know she was not married yet. It sounded as though she was engaged, so she was not free to pursue anything with Matthew, but at least she still had time to choose.

Matthew let go of her hand and stood up to pace the room behind the sofa. Claire was not married, but she was still off-limits. The woman had a fiancé who was coming in the morning to claim her.

"Are you sure they're legit? They aren't someone who's out to take her for nefarious reasons?" John, of all people, asked.

The sheriff turned around and faced the room. "I trust the sheriff in Red Creek. But that's why I've asked they come to the sheriff's station in town so I can verify in person before I tell them where Claire is. They're goin' ta bring your passport and a few other personal items to verify ya really are their daughter and fiancé."

Claire rubbed her hands on her thighs. He'd said *fiancé* again, meaning she was still free to choose. "Thank you, Sheriff. What time will you expect me to come in?"

Roscoe shook his head. "I don't want you comin' ta town until I've verified it myself. How 'bout I call out here once I'm sure and we can decide where to go from there? They can come out here, or you can come to town. Whichever is more comfortable for you."

Claire nodded.

"Roscoe, I'd prefer it if they came out here. I'd like to meet them and help ensure that they're on the up 'n up before we let them take our Claire." Caleb, as head of the household, had laid claim to Claire as one of the family and he was not about to let her go without seeing the proof for himself. Especially if she still did not have her memory.

The sheriff nodded. "Of course." He turned to Claire. "Do you mind if I bring them out here?"

Claire sighed and felt more secure with the idea of them coming out here, to a place where she felt safe and wanted. She still was not sure what sort of family would let their daughter run away and not try to find her for a week. But she would find out tomorrow.

CHAPTER 22

She had not slept well. In fact, Claire doubted she'd had more than an hour of sleep. All sorts of scenarios ran through her head, from what type of people her family were to why she ran.

At least she knew she ran and was not abducted. Although, she had never really thought much of that idea.

Running away on a horse was a bit melodramatic, even for her. Maybe she was a different sort of woman before she lost her memory? She hoped she was not a drama queen. What she and Brad had fought about would not come to her. She tried, and got a headache for her troubles. Thankfully, it was not as bad as they were in the beginning. Which made her think that she might be getting closer to recovering her memory.

While she enjoyed the Sunday service and had appreciated the prayers all week, she was not sure if she was the praying sort. Sunday night while she was getting ready for bed, she thought about God. She wondered if she was a believer, and something inside her calmed her thoughts and told her not to worry—she was a child of God.

It was as though she was communing with the Holy Spirit in her room, and she felt a peace that passed all understanding. She was going to ask about it Monday night after dinner, but with the sheriff's bombshell news, she did not have time to think about that again.

When she was alone Monday night, she got down on her knees next to her bed and prayed for the first time, that she could remember, all on her own. Claire had asked God for direction and protection. The peace she felt earlier in the day had been shattered, so she requested more peace.

Off and on all night she found herself talking to God and telling him how she felt and asking him to restore her memory. While she still could not remember, at least she had an idea of who she was. She knew that she could trust Sheriff Roscoe to ensure those people really were her family, and he would not have come out to see her if he had any doubts.

The fact that he was still asking them to bring proof when they showed up added more comfort for Claire. If they had sent a fake passport, the sheriff would know.

All she had to do was trust him to protect her. Since the sheriff had seen through Scott's lies before anyone else, she knew she could put her trust in the lawman. But that did not mean she would not be asking her own questions and ensuring that she took the phone number for the ranch with her. If anything seemed wrong when she left, she would be calling them for help.

For now, she would follow the sheriff's lead and have an open mind.

Since Claire could not sleep, she figured she might as well get up early and help Judith with breakfast for the last time.

The sun was just peeking above the horizon, and it took Claire's breath away. The oranges mixed with the white of the low-lying clouds gave her peace. It was almost as though God had painted a picture just for her. He knew exactly what her mind needed to calm itself and enjoy the view.

When she peeked out of her window, she heard the unmistakable crowing of a rooster. Funny, she had not heard him once since she'd arrived. Or had she just slept so hard she missed the fowl's morning wake-up calls?

A slow smile spread across her face when she realized it must not have crowed on her side of the house. People thought farm animals were dumb, but she knew better. The rooster had let her sleep since she needed it for recovery.

A wisp of a memory blew through her mind, and she thought of a black dog with long, shaggy fur loving up against her legs. She could not place the time, but it had to be recent since she had those turquoise boots on in the memory. His name was out of reach, but she tried anyway. A light headache started at her left temple, and she decided to let it go. Getting a headache today of all days was not worth it.

She would have to ask her family about the dog and see what they said. Maybe that could be her way of ensuring they were the correct family.

Claire had not been up this early since she arrived, so she was surprised when she entered the kitchen and it was empty. A lone light shone above the coffee maker, but that was it. There was still a little bit of coffee in the pot. When she touched it, she realized it was only lukewarm. "So, the Mannings really do get up early." She shook her head and began to make a fresh pot of coffee.

It was not long before she was sitting at the kitchen table looking out the window with the yellow gingham curtains. A bittersweet pang filled her chest when she realized this would be her last morning to enjoy a cup of hot coffee and look out that window to the back paddock.

Even though she had only been here a week, she would miss this place. She doubted her own home felt this comfortable and right. A lone tear slowly made its way down her cheek. Instead of wiping it away, she let it mark her face as she closed her eyes and prayed the Lord would protect her that day as well as tell her what she needed to do.

"Claire?" Judith's surprised voice startled her, and she turned to see the woman turning on the lights. "What are you doing up so early?"

"I couldn't sleep. I hope you don't mind that I was in here so early." Claire brought up her coffee mug to show Judith what she had been up to before taking a sip.

"Of course not. You know you're welcome to go wherever you want." Judith walked over to the table and took a seat next to Claire. She picked up the younger woman's hand and squeezed it. "Nervous about today?"

Claire could not speak. A dry knot enveloped her esophagus, and she had to focus in order to just breath. Her hand squeezed the coffee mug, and she nodded.

Judith stood and walked to the counter with the coffee pot. "I think that's normal. I'd be surprised if you weren't nervous or anxious for today."

"Yeah, I guess." Claire shrugged before taking a long sip of her hot coffee.

"Would you like to help me with breakfast today? I was planning on making something special for you." Judith had not made her special pancakes yet, and she knew today was the right day to do so.

"Sure, how can I help?" Claire sat up straighter and decided it would not do her any good to think more about the people she might meet that day. Instead, she needed to focus on the Manning family and doing her part to help their day.

"Can you grab five pounds of bacon from the fridge on

the back porch?" Judith called over her shoulder as she put the coffee pot back on the warmer.

"Sure." Claire smiled, thinking about the applewood-smoked bacon Judith had made the other day. They got their pork from a neighbor, who did the smoking before exchanging it for some of the Triple J beef.

Since she had been there, Claire learned that a lot of the ranchers traded goods with each other. While most families had small herb and vegetable gardens, they needed more than they could grow. There was a thriving trade taking place in Beacon Creek. And every Saturday some of the local farmers and ranchers went up to Bozeman for a local farmers' market.

Beacon Creek had a little market where they could buy groceries, but most of the farmers and ranchers used freshly grown vegetables or meat that was butchered locally. There were not a lot of fruit farmers, so they did buy fruit from the grocery along with other goods like flour, sugar, and so forth.

Claire had even seen a few frozen pizzas in the Mannings' deep freezer. They must have had those when Judith did not feel like cooking. But since Claire had been there, Judith had lovingly prepared all three meals each day.

Without knowing what time the sheriff would be coming out, Claire figured this would be her last meal with the family. She was going to enjoy it and not let the impending move back to wherever she came from spoil breakfast.

Once she had the bacon in her hands, she returned to the kitchen and set to work frying it. Since they had to make so much, she used all four burners to make the flavorful meat while Judith pulled out an electric skillet and put out the hash browns to cook on it.

While Claire turned the bacon and checked to ensure they browned evenly, Judith whipped up pancakes. And just before she poured them onto the electric skillet, she took off the cooked hash browns and put them into the oven to stay warm.

Once the batter was on the newly cleaned electric skillet, Judith added chocolate chips to each circle.

Claire could not remember if she liked chocolate chip pancakes, but she certainly couldn't wait to try them.

Once the current batch of bacon was done, Claire pulled them off and put them on a large platter with paper towels to help dry off the extra grease. Then she emptied the skillets of the grease and added more bacon. They would need it if past mornings were any indication. Five pounds of bacon may have seemed like an extreme amount, but with the entire Manning house eating breakfast together, and all but two of them hardworking ranch men, they'd want plenty of bacon to fill their bellies for the day ahead.

Not to mention, bacon. Even Claire knew all men loved bacon with a passion.

Once everyone was seated and the platters put on the table, Mr. Manning prayed over the food. The women were first to get bacon, as everyone at that table knew that there would be none left once the men dug in.

Claire's first bite of the creamy goodness that was a chocolate chip pancake slathered in syrup had her moaning. "Oh.My.Goodness," Claire said as she slowly chewed her first bit of heaven.

Everyone around the table laughed and continued to eat their meal. No one was talking, as everyone loved the chocolate chip pancakes with bacon.

After a few bites of the pancake, Claire took a piece of bacon from her plate that had syrup on it and ate it. She knew she would never have forgotten having something so heavenly as chocolate chip pancakes. She could not have forgotten the way her belly felt when the food went down. Her taste buds continued to thank her as she put more food into her mouth.

This was one meal she would be making herself on a regular basis. She did not care how full of sugar it was, she'd need this bit of comfort after she left the Triple J.

A frown crept up on Claire's face and she put her silverware down on her plate with a clunk.

"What's wrong?" Matthew whispered when he noticed how unhappy Claire appeared.

"Nothing."

"Then why are you frowning? And why did you stop eating? Surely you aren't full yet?" Matthew wanted to reach out and take her last piece of bacon if she was full. But he waited to hear what Claire said before he took it.

A wry smile crossed Claire's face. "No, I'm not full."

"Then what's wrong?" Matthew had an idea, but he wanted to hear Claire say it.

"I'm not really sure." She took a bite, knowing she was sure but not wanting to say it out loud. "Can we go for one last ride after breakfast?"

Matthew sat back in his seat and let out a breath. He had hoped they could, but he was not sure she would be up for it. "Yes, of course we can."

Claire nodded and went back to eating.

When everyone was done, Mr. Manning looked to Claire. "I know this is most likely your last breakfast with us, but I want ya to know that you're always welcome here." He cleared his throat and tried not to let any emotion show through his words. "You're part of our family. We all wanted you to know that, Claire."

Caleb picked up his coffee mug, and the rest of the family joined him. They all said they agreed with their pa and began clinking their mugs as though they were drinking sparkling cider on New Year's Eve and toasting in the New Year.

Claire felt the tears prick the backs of her eyes, but she bit her lip to keep from crying. The last thing she needed was to come off weak in front of all these men. She was going to be strong and thankful for the limited time she had with a wonderful family. One she knew would go after her if she had disappeared from them.

"Thank you all. I have loved my time here. I want to stay in touch." She looked at Judith and smiled. "I hope that if any of you are ever in my neck of the woods, wherever that may be…" She laughed, and everyone at the table joined her. "I hope you know you'll always be welcome wherever I live."

Everyone clinked mugs again and sent up *hear, hears*, and, *you bets* before taking gulps of their drinks.

Claire stood up and began clearing away the dishes. Mark walked over to her and took the plates out of her hand. "Here, let me do this." He nodded to Matthew. "You two go for a ride. I think Whiskers wants to see you before you leave." He smiled knowingly at her before turning to take the dirty plates to the sink.

"Thanks, Mark. Will I see you all again before I leave?" All of a sudden, a heavy feeling hit her and she worried she'd never see this family again.

"You better say goodbye before takin' off." John stood up and gave her a stern look.

"If y'all are around, then I will." She nodded and smiled at them all, taking one last look at the only family she could remember, for now.

"Oh, we will be. Count on it," Caleb said before helping his wife finish clearing the dishes.

Matthew led Claire outside. When they were inside the barn and away from prying eyes, he asked, "How ya feelin'?"

She huffed. "How do you think? I'm nervous and unsure."

"Unsure?" Matthew furrowed his brows.

She walked to where Whiskers stood with her head over the stall door, waiting for Claire to pet her and probably give her a treat.

She had not thought to bring carrots with her. After their ride, she would have to give Whiskers an extra scoop of grain as a way of thanking her for the love and attention the horse had shown her since they first met.

With her hand on her the horse's mane, she answered him, "Yeah. I don't know what to think about this. What if they aren't my real family? Will we know? And what if they are? Will I ever get my memory back?"

He had feared the same things. When he walked closer to her, without even thinking he pulled her into his body and wrapped her up with his arms. The last thing he wanted was for Claire to be upset, or unsure about the family coming to claim her.

"Shhh. Don't worry. The sheriff will know for sure. Let's not borrow trouble before it's due." Matthew did not want to think about the possible issues, or even her leaving. All he wanted was to spend the rest of the time he had with her riding and talking. He wanted his last memory to be happy, not sad. And he wanted her to remember him fondly.

Claire wrapped her arms around Matthew's waist and turned her head into his big, broad chest, setting her head under his chin. She was exactly where she wanted to be. She did not want to leave his arms. Not now, not ever. But...

"Will we see each other again?" The whispered words left her lips without her consciously speaking them.

He tightened his hold on her and closed his eyes. Her scent enveloped him and he felt his heart breaking. Exactly what his mother did not want. He did not want it either, but he'd never regret meeting Claire and spending this time with her.

"I hope so. You heard Pa, you're part of this family and always welcome here." Even if she came back with her husband, he would be happy to welcome her back. No matter how much it hurt to even think of her with another man.

They stood there holding each other for a few more moments before Matthew pulled back and looked down into Claire's eyes. The tension between them was strong, and he felt a need to kiss her.

But his head and heart were warring with each other. She was engaged, even if she could not remember the man. So he couldn't do that to her. It would be wrong to put her in that position.

Claire looked up into Matthew's eyes and felt her heart flittering and her stomach roiling like a storm on the sea. She wanted his lips on hers, but should she? Could she? She was not married, but she was engaged. Or at least, she had been told she was engaged. Running away from her fiancé the day of her wedding—while in her dress, no less—could mean she was not.

Her heart told her to stand on her tippy-toes and bring her lips to his. But her mind said until she dealt with her fiancé and knew exactly what was going on, she had no right to kiss another man, even if she could not remember the man she was supposed to be kissing.

Her memories would come. She knew it.

With the headaches easing and memories starting to have a bit more form to them, they would come.

But when Matthew looked so intently into her eyes, all thought fled, and her body leaned closer toward him.

Matthew saw her look at his lips, and he looked at hers.

Everything inside him screamed to kiss the girl. But something in the back of his mind told him now was not the time. She was not his filly; she belonged to another man.

When he felt himself bending his head and his eyes locked on her lips, he made a last-minute change and lightly pressed a kiss to her temple.

CHAPTER 23

It was not what Claire wanted, but she would take it. His soft lips on her temple had her feeling like she was floating on those white, fluffy clouds she'd seen in the sky on her way to the barn. If Matthew had not been holding her in his arms, she knew her legs would have given out on her.

Any nearness to the cowboy who made her feel things she doubted she had ever felt before was something she wanted to hold onto with every fiber of her being.

She knew he was right in pulling back at the last minute. Even she knew she could not let him kiss her, not until she met this Brad fellow and they discussed what went wrong and where they were going from here.

And until she regained her memories, she could not choose a different man, no matter how much she ached for him. It would not be fair to anyone involved if one day she woke up and remembered exactly who she was, and that she had been in love with another man.

She cleared her throat and pulled back once she had her balance back. "I think we should get moving if we're going to be back before the sheriff shows up."

Matthew could not believe he had kissed her. Well, kissed her temple. But still, that was no sisterly kiss.

"Of course, I'll grab the saddle and be right back." He did not want her following him to the tack room and the two of them being alone in such a tight space. He doubted he would be able to pull himself back again.

The rush of feelings for this little filly when he heard the sheriff notify her she was not married must have gone to his head. She was still engaged, and he would need to remember that.

When he came back out with Whiskers' saddle in his arms, Claire was stroking the horse's mane and neck. He walked around to the other side of the horse and set the saddle down on the fence before putting the blanket on the horse's back.

Without a word, they worked together to saddle both horses and then they led them out of the barn to where they had a mounting block. As much as Matthew wanted to be the one to help Claire mount her horse, he could not imagine putting his hands on her waist and *not* kissing her for real.

When they had been riding for at least ten minutes, Claire took in a deep breath and looked around. She took in the scenery, the scents, and how she felt being on the Triple J Ranch. The pang in her heart returned, and she turned away from Matthew so he could not see the tears coming down her face.

She picked up the pace and galloped through the pastures, leading them both. After a few more minutes she wondered if she could choose to stay there with Matthew and his family. Would her family put up a fight? Should she do something like that?

Once the thought entered her mind, she could not keep it from growing. She led them toward the little picnic area next to the stream. Once they were there, she dismounted and tied Whiskers to a tree.

Matthew followed her without a word. When they were both seated on a bench, she turned to him.

"What if I decided to stay?" Hope filled her chest, and she looked expectantly at Matthew.

Pain crossed his features before he schooled them and looked out over the water in the stream as it bubbled past them. "Do you think you'd regret not getting to know your family?"

He had thought about it during their ride, but then he decided that she would eventually regret it and possibly hold him responsible for not choosing her family. This was probably the hardest thing he had ever done in his life. And he doubted he would ever do anything more difficult, but he had to encourage her to go home and try to get her memory back.

She turned away from him, and when he heard her sniff, he felt like a fool.

"I'm sorry, Claire. I want you to stay, I do. But that's me being selfish." He scooted closer and put one arm around her shoulders.

She leaned into him and sighed. "You do?"

He pulled back and grabbed ahold of her shoulders. "Of course I do. But you're engaged to another man and have a family you can't remember yet." He let go of her and pulled his hat off before he ran a ragged hand through his hair. Then he stood up and rubbed his hand down his face. "Claire, you need to get your memory back before you make any big decisions."

He may not be a doctor or even a genius, but even he knew that.

"What if I don't want my memory back? Did you ever stop and think that I might have forgotten my life for a good reason?" Claire jumped up and began to pace in front of the picnic bench. "Who knows what type of people they are!" She threw her hands in the air and huffed.

With a shaky hand, he rubbed his face and nodded. "What say you we wait until you meet them? They may have a good reason for lettin' you run."

She put her fisted hands on her hips. "Really? You think good parents could possibly have a good reason for letting their daughter run away on her wedding day without chasing after her? Please, tell me what that could be."

He was infuriating! First, he acted as though he wanted to kiss her, then he kissed her forehead, and now he was making excuses for her absentee family. Was there something about her that caused people to not care very much for her?

She was not ready to accept they had a good reason. Nor was she ready to resume her old life. Especially when she still did not know what all that entailed.

Matthew sighed and took hold of her hand.

Claire jumped.

"Come on, let's head back home. I'll bet they're waitin' for us already." He did not want to let her go, but what was that old saying? Let something go, and if it was meant to be, it'd come back you? No, that was not it.

He snapped his fingers and whispered, "That's it."

Claire's brows furrowed. "What's it?"

"Oh, nothing. Sorry, I'm having a tough time concentrating." He pursed his lips and told himself quietly, *If you love something, set it free. If it comes back it's yours. If it doesn't, it was never meant to be.* He would have to tell himself that again and again. Until his heart believed it. Or until Claire returned.

Hopefully, the latter.

CHAPTER 24

The sheriff was waiting for them when they returned to the barn. Thankfully, he was standing there alone.

"Does this mean they didn't check out?" Hope was a dangerous thing to hold onto, but Claire felt this might be her last chance.

The sheriff sighed and looked down. "I'm sorry. I'm not sure what you were hoping for, but they did check out. Your parents and your…"—he looked between the couple who'd just dismounted from their horses—"fiancé, are inside waiting for you."

If her heart had not already been breaking, it would have crashed with a huge bang and the shards of it would have flown in a thousand different pieces. As it was, she hung her head and took a deep breath. This was what she'd both feared and hoped for.

At least now she would know.

Claire and Matthew followed the sheriff inside to the living room, where everyone was gathered along with three strangers.

Or were they?

Claire bent over in pain, put her hands to her temples, and sucked in a quick breath.

Matthew leaned over and wrapped her in his arms. "Are you alright? What's wrong, Claire?"

A tall, dark-haired man stood up. "Let go of my fiancé." He stalked toward Matthew and Claire, and the sheriff got between them.

"Hold up, Mr. Brown. Claire's in pain and he's helping her. Your attitude isn't going to help matters one bit." Roscoe put his hand in front of the obviously upset man.

The man pointed to Matthew. "What's wrong with her?"

Judith carefully walked over and stood beside Claire. "Surely you know she has amnesia?" She widened her eyes and waited for the man to speak.

Brad Brown was not nearly as tall as Matthew, but he was taller than Claire. He stood at five feet ten inches with black hair and brown eyes. He was not a cowboy, or at least he was not wearing the clothing of a cowboy.

Instead, he wore a suit and tie with shiny, fancy shoes that did not look the least bit comfortable to Matthew. Give him a pair of leather boots any day and he would be happy.

Matthew could not help but wonder what Claire saw in the man. While he could understand the jealous, possessive act of a fiancé, he did not think the two of them made a good couple. Not at all. They were complete opposites. And not in the opposites-attract sort of way.

From what Matthew could see, Brad was a corporate suit while Claire was a true cowgirl. Probably even a horse trainer. How they had gotten together baffled him.

"Let me help her." Brad tried to muscle his way in to take hold of his fiancé.

Claire held up a hand. "Brad, back off," she huffed out before standing and glaring at him.

While Brad had gone all caveman on Matthew, who only wanted to help her, she had an extremely intense barrage of memories cramming back into her brain and causing more pain than she had felt since she woke up a week ago.

When she stood up, her eyes skimmed the room until she stopped on the other newcomers. "Mom, Dad." She nodded in their direction.

Judith beamed and put a hand on Claire's shoulder. "Do you remember them?"

"Yes, and I have a lot of questions for everyone." She scowled at Brad, who took two steps back.

"Everything?" he asked in a hushed tone.

Claire narrowed her eyes. "Everything."

Brad nervously licked his lips and looked around at the way everyone was glaring at him. He knew Claire could not have remembered what he did before that moment, otherwise he doubted they would have let him in the house.

"Can we go somewhere private and discuss this?" While her parents knew what happened, they had not said much to him. He was rather surprised they allowed him to follow them to Beacon Creek. They did refuse to let him ride with them, and when they stopped for gas and food, they basically ignored him.

He could not blame them. Brad wished he could cut himself out of his own life, too.

He owed her an explanation and an apology. While there was no excuse for what he did, he needed to see if they could repair the damage and move forward together.

Brad held his hand out for Claire, but she crossed her arms over her chest and glared at him. "I can't believe you dared come here after what you did. Did you think I wouldn't remember?"

He shook his head. This was going all wrong. "No, that's not it at all. I had to come and see you. See if you were alright." Brad looked around again and sighed. "And apologize. I'd really rather do this with no one else around, if that's alright with you?"

She looked into his pleading eyes and she felt nothing. Not even the hatred she had felt when she first fled. "Fine, but I want my parents in the room when we talk. They need to know, if they don't already." She turned her heated gaze to them. "I have a few questions for you as well."

Her mom's shoulders sagged, and she wiped a tear from her cheek. "Of course, dear."

Claire led the visitors to the front room and sat in one of the recliners, not giving anyone a chance to sit next to her.

Once everyone was seated, she looked around and her eyes stopped on her parents, who were sitting on a sofa together, holding hands. "Why didn't you look for me when I ran away?"

Her mother broke out in a sob and her father put his arms around his wife. "Claire. Don't be like that."

"Like what, Dad? Like a daughter who has spent the past week without a memory and afraid her own family wasn't looking for her?" Apparently, Claire did still have some pent-up anger left in her after all.

"Honey, we called all of your friends. Even a few of your clients. No one had heard from you. When we were about to call the sheriff, Brad finally told us what happened." Richard Stapleton glared at the man who broke his daughter's heart. "Once we learned what happened, we figured you needed time to be alone. Since you didn't have any money, your truck, or even a phone, we figured you went to a friend's house who kept your presence there a secret." Richard realized he had made a mistake, but he never thought his own daughter would doubt she was loved by her parents.

"Really? You thought I was hiding from you?" She chuckled.

Karen Stapleton, her mother, sat up straight and wiped the tears from her eyes. "I'm so sorry, dear. I thought about what you went through and felt that if it had been me, I'd want a few days alone. I was ready to call the sheriff in on Monday morning when Snickers came home." She broke out in tears again, and her husband held her tighter.

"Sweetheart, we really did think you were alright. I know now that we made a huge mistake in not going after you right away." Her dad glared at Brad, who sat in the chair next to Claire and across from him and his wife.

"What happened to you? How did you end up without your horse and a gash on your head that caused you amnesia?" Karen had worried non-stop about her daughter's health since the moment she heard the details of how she was found along the side of the road.

She looked her daughter over from head to toe and did not see anything other than bags under her eyes. There may have been a few scratches on Claire's hands, but that was normal for her daughter. She did work a ranch all day, every day.

"I had Snickers going at full gallop and a truck passed us by and honked its horn. Even though I was on the side of the road, in the dirt at least five feet away from the edge of the blacktop, the noise must have startled him and he reared up." Claire rubbed the side of her head. "I couldn't stay on and fell off. I hit my head on a rock or something and blacked out. When I came to, there was not anything around. Not even Snickers." Her poor horse must have been spooked beyond measure. "Is he alright?"

Her dad nodded and released a nervous chuckle. "Yes, he had some scrapes and threw a shoe, but Gus took good care of him. I'm sure by the time we get back, he'll be excited to see you and want to desperately apologize for leaving you injured on the side of the road."

Claire nodded. "I'm glad he's alright. Sounds like he did better than me. At least he remembered where home was, even if it did take him so long to get there."

She still had a little bit of a headache. Although, it was almost gone; now it was more like a phantom pain than anything else. The pain was not in her temples, it was along the side of her head, under her hair, where she had the gash from the fall. Claire put a light hand to the spot and winced. The only time it really hurt after the first few days was when she brushed her hair, or touched it. Like now.

"Claire, the most important thing to remember is that we love you. Your mother and I were worried and several times were about to call in the sheriff, but then we thought about why you ran and realized it wouldn't do any good if you were hiding out with a friend." Her father looked at her with all the love in his eyes she knew he felt for her.

She nodded. "I know, Dad." She sat there thinking for a moment before saying, "I think it was probably the right thing to do. I was on my way to a friend's house. Someone none of you would have thought to contact." She bit her lower lip.

Now that all of her memories were back, she was beginning to process the events leading up to her departure, as well as what had happened after she arrived in Beacon Creek. She could not blame her parents. In fact, they did the right thing. Had they called the sheriff, her face and the fact she ran out on her fiancé right before their wedding would have been all over the news.

"How did the sheriff locate me so quickly?" She cringed.

"Is it all over the news now?" The last thing she and her horse-training business needed was this sort of negative publicity. It wouldn't matter why she ran, they'd just hear about the running part. Then she would lose business.

"Actually, he was about to put out an all-points bulletin when he found the social media post. I'm actually surprised none of our friends found it first. But maybe no one was really looking for you?" Karen shrugged and pulled away from her husband's arms.

"Then what does everyone think about me? Where I am?" Claire knew that even though her wedding was small, people still knew about it. The fact that it was supposed to happen on a Tuesday helped to keep it small. Which was exactly what she wanted.

"They think you went on your trip to Texas. Brad's stayed quiet and indoors ever since. Those who do know have all promised to keep it quiet." The stern look in her father's eyes told her why everyone had agreed to keep mum on this bit of juicy gossip.

It also helped that most people liked her more than they did Brad. He was a very likeable guy, but he was not a cowboy. Where she was from, you were either a cowboy or not. Part of the reason they were going to marry was to add legitimacy to his family ranch, as well as the money the Browns so desperately needed.

Her marriage was supposed to be more of a business arrangement than a love match. But Claire had hoped they would both choose to love each other, and love would become part of their marriage, in time.

She turned her steely-eyed gaze to her fiancé and glared at him. "Why did you cheat on me with my own cousin? I mean come on, how cliché could it be—you and the brides-maid?" Claire stood up and paced to the window of the smaller room and looked outside. She couldn't bring herself to look at Brad any more.

Brad ran a hand over his face and blew out a deep breath. "I am so sorry. I never meant for you to find out like that."

Claire whirled around. "Like that? What do you mean? You never meant for me to find out at all, did you?" She pointed a finger at him and narrowed her eyes.

He gulped and looked at the ground, the gravity of what he had done truly hitting him there. Before that moment, he thought they might actually be able to salvage things. It was what his family needed and expected of him.

"I was saying goodbye."

"How long were you having an affair with Gina?" She put her hands on her hips and waited for him to answer her.

"Almost six months." He knew it was wrong. He never should have spent time alone with the beautiful blonde. She was Claire's total opposite, and she had always liked him. He did not know it until they started working together, and then one night when they were working late in the office, things sort of got out of control and he kissed her.

Brad knew it was wrong, but since the engagement was not between two people who loved each other, he did not think it was so bad. It was only a kiss, after all. Had it stopped right then and there, it probably would not have been a big deal.

Working with Gina every day, her living on his ranch, and the way she made him feel, he could not help but kiss her again one day when they were in the pool. She had on a string bikini and he could not help himself. She wanted him, and he wanted to know what it felt like to kiss a woman he had romantic feelings for.

At first, that was all it was—a stolen kiss here and there.

Then it turned into dates, and last month it went too far. He had fallen in love with her and he could not stop himself. She had fallen in love with him years ago and wanted it all with him. Even though Gina knew he was marrying Claire, she said she wanted his love right up until the day he married Claire.

They had agreed that everything would stop once he was married. She was going to move out so they would not be tempted.

"Six months?" Claire slumped down into her chair and stared out into nothingness. "You love her, don't you?"

Claire knew when it started—right after they announced their engagement. Not two weeks later he began to pull back from her and they rarely did anything together. She could probably count on one hand the amount of dates they'd had, and the kisses had all but stopped.

She thought about it and counted in her head. Now that she had her memory back, it all made sense. "You stopped kissing me right after we were engaged. I wondered about it, but we were both so busy, and I knew you weren't in love with me."

"What?" Her father about blew his lid. Richard jumped up and put a finger in Brad's face. "You never even loved my little girl?"

Karen put a hand on her husband's arm. "Richard, I don't think this is the place for this conversation. We should go home and discuss it there."

Mr. and Mrs. Manning entered the room together and looked around.

"Is everything alright?" Judith asked politely. While she did not want to get in the middle of a family discussion, she also did not want anyone to fight in her house. She was a bit worried about what she had heard so far. Not that she was eavesdropping, but it was a bit tough to close off one's ears when someone was yelling so loudly.

Richard took two steps back and fisted his hands at his sides. "Forgive me. I shouldn't have had this conversation here. We'll take our daughter and go. Thank you so much for taking such good care of our little girl. I don't know what I would have done if we'd never found her."

Part of Richard was so angry at not going looking for his daughter right away. He only had himself to blame over that part. But the rest of it, he was going to have to work very hard to keep from boxing Brad into the next county. He never liked violence, but the paternal part of him needed to do something to prove to his family he cared for his daughter and would not stand by and let some cheating man-whore hurt her.

Claire's cheeks burned with embarrassment. Her father had never lost his lid like that before. She did not know what Brad had told them, but it sounded as though it was not much. Even she did not know much, other than what she had seen.

It was no wonder her mind would not let her remember her life. It was all a lie. Sure, she knew why he was marrying her, but she had no clue that he had been cheating on her. She guessed she should have paid more attention to everything going on around her. Hindsight and all that…

"I only have a few things I want to take with me. And I want to thank the Mannings and say goodbye to them before leaving." She hugged her mother and father and completely ignored Brad. She would deal with him when she got home.

"Claire, I'll be waiting for you in the car." Brad looked at her hesitantly, perhaps hopefully.

"Pft. Not on your life. If I get into a small space like a car with you right now, I'm liable to cause an accident. No." She pursed her lips and pointed to the front door. "Get yourself home and I'll talk to you when I've cooled down."

"But Claire, we need to talk." He did not want her going home without hearing the entire story. He had to tell her everything.

"No, Brad. It's all your fault we're in this predicament, you can wait until *I'm* ready to talk." Claire walked past him and into the family room, where all the family had been waiting for her.

"Come on, Brad. Let's give her some time to say her goodbyes to the family who took care of her when we couldn't." Karen pulled his arm and led him out the front door.

Richard stopped and turned back to the Mannings. "Thank you so much for taking care of our little girl. I don't know how we got where we are, but I can promise you, it won't happen again."

Mr. Manning put out his hand and Richard shook it. "Feel free to call me if you need any help. I mean it."

Richard nodded his gratitude and followed his wife to their truck.

Brad was already inside his car.

Caleb watched them from the front door before closing it. He shook his head and wondered how a cow patty such as Brad could have gotten Claire to agree to marry him. He did not even drive a truck! Or wear a hat, or boots. That man wore suits, for Pete's sake. What sort of rancher wore suits? None who actually worked their own ranch, he knew that for certain.

Once Claire was confident her family and Brad were outside, she sighed, and her shoulders drooped. She rubbed her forehead. "Maybe it would have been better not to remember."

Matthew wanted nothing more than to take his little filly in his arms and hold her tight and never let go. He had no clue how he was going to say goodbye to Claire. He did not think he would ever be able to say goodbye to the woman who had stolen his heart.

CHAPTER 25

Tears pricked the backs of Claire's eyes, but she was not going to let them fall. Not yet.

"I'm so sorry for that scene." Claire waved to the front room, where she had just had a horrendous encounter with Brad. While she did not know what she was going to do about him, she knew she had to get home. Horses, and people, were waiting for her.

But she did not want to leave. Not yet.

"Where are you from?" Mark asked. They had not really gotten any questions answered about who Claire was, only that her lying, no good, cheating fiancé seemed to expect her to go home with him.

Claire rubbed her face with both hands and took a seat in one of the recliners. "I'm from a small town about three hours from here, Red Creek. You ever heard of it?"

They all nodded.

"As a matter of fact, I drove by it the day I found you." Matthew sat on the sofa across from her. He was glad she took a single seat. He would have wanted to sit by her if she sat on the sofa, and that would not have been good for either of them.

Claire's fingers itched to touch Matthew, but she could not. Not yet. "That makes sense, I suppose."

"Isn't anyone here goin' ta say it?" John asked.

Everyone looked upon John with confusion written on their faces.

John sighed. "She obviously doesn't *have* to leave. She can stay here." He pointed to the only woman he had ever seen make his brother smile like he had the past week, and he wanted her to stay. Claire made the entire house happy. If she left… He did not even want to think about that possibility.

The tears pricking at the backs of Claire's eyes would not obey, and they began to fall. "Thank you, John. I really appreciate that. But"—she looked around the room—"I do have to go home. I have horses relying on me, as well as clients." She stood up and walked to the window overlooking the back area next to the paddock.

"But if your place is only three hours away, you could work from here. Go back, get your stuff, and come back here, where you belong." John was not going to let her go back to that cheater. Especially after he heard that the pair were not even in love. Who married someone in this day and age *without* love?

Mr. Manning, who looked upon Claire as one of his own, agreed with John. "Yes, I hope you know that you'll always have a place here in our home. If you want to work from here, we'll make plenty of room for you. What is it, exactly, that you do?"

Claire turned around and wrapped her arms around her middle. "I train horses." She looked to Matthew, and they shared a knowing smile. It was one of the occupations they had discussed as a possibility, considering how well she interacted with their horses.

"You could train them here," Matthew offered.

When Claire wiped the tears from her cheeks, Judith ushered the family out of the room. "Let's give them some time to speak. How about coffee?"

Everyone followed the matriarch of the house into the kitchen.

Claire walked to Matthew and took his hands in hers. "I can't tell you how grateful I am, and always will be, for this time with you and your family. I highly doubt anyone else would have taken such great care of me." She chuckled. "I doubt anyone honest would have offered to bring me home with them other than your family."

He shook his head. "You'd be surprised by how many folks in the area would have stepped up to help."

"Maybe. But I do need to get going." She did not want to leave, but with so many waiting for her return, and the situation with Brad, she had to deal with everything first.

"Why can't you come back here? Bring your horses, there's plenty of room for you to train. If we need to erect a new barn, we can. We can do anything you need to bring your business here." Matthew wanted her close by so he could properly court her. If she was three hours away, he might see her once a week at best. Probably less than that.

Not wanting to give him false hope, and not wanting to explain the entire situation, she pulled her hands away. "I'm sorry. I do need to get home, and I'll have a lot to deal with. Maybe we can stay in touch?"

That was not what Matthew wanted. He wanted her close by. The way she spoke, it sounded like Claire was not interested in anything other than a casual friendship. How could he have thought a woman like her would want him once she got her memory back?

It finally clicked who she was—Claire Stapleton. She was one of the best horse trainers in the country, and worth a pretty penny, too. While he and his family were not poor, they certainly were not rich. Not like the Stapletons. They had horses that went for astronomical amounts at auction. They also trained some of the finest racehorses in the country. She was so far out of his league, she might as well be in another solar system.

And she was leaving.

"Right. Well, I wish you well. If you're ever in this area, stop by. I'm sure my family would love to see you." Matthew was not going to let her see how much this hurt him. He did have some pride. Even after she had shredded it with her refusal to stay after he practically begged her.

Claire winced at Matthew's tone. She really did want to keep in touch, but she did not know yet how much she could offer him of herself. While she wanted to give him her whole heart, she was not in a position to do so.

"If it's alright, I'd like to get the sweater from my room?" She did not need it, or anything else. She had an entire closet full of clothes back home, but something about that sweater made her feel at home when she had first arrived. Plus, it would always remind her of her time here with the Manning family, and Matthew.

He nodded, not able to speak for fear of saying something stupid.

She turned to leave the room, then stopped at the doorway. Looking back over her shoulder, she smiled one last time at Matthew. "Thank you for being a true friend. Now that I have my memory back, I know that's a very rare gift."

Matthew returned her smile—how could he not? But it did not reach his eyes, just like hers did not reach her eyes.

Claire grabbed the sweater from the back of the chair it had been hung on the night before and she took one last look around. It really was a nice room. One she would miss when she was gone. Something out the window caught her attention, and she walked across the room.

A chuckle escaped her lips when she saw the bright-red comb of the rooster waving at her. Well, it was not exactly waving, but it appeared as though the rooster who let her sleep in when she needed it was saying goodbye. Claire lifted a hand and waved at the rooster, who pecked his way back around to the other side of the house. Once he was out of sight, she turned and left the room to find the rest of the family.

Saying goodbye should not have been so hard, but it was. After only the second hug, she was crying again and still had Judith to hug goodbye. When she got to the woman who had served not only as her caregiver for the past week, but also a surrogate mom, she was a mess.

"I'm really going to miss you, Judith. I hope you know how much I've appreciated my time here with you, in particular." Claire wiped her nose on her sleeve, and Caleb pulled a clean handkerchief out of his pocket and handed it to her.

Claire smiled at the gentleman cowboy. "Thank you." She blew her nose and wiped her face. When she went to hand it back to him, he waved her off, telling her to keep it. She would have to wash it and then send it back. Maybe she could even use it as an excuse to come back for a visit.

Judith pulled Claire into a tight hug. "You come back now, ya hear? You're part of this family now, and don't you go forgettin' it."

They both laughed when they realized the unintended pun.

Claire nodded. "I will. And you are always welcome at the Stapleton ranch. Your entire family will be treated like ours. I hope you can come visit sometime soon."

Judith and Caleb walked Claire to the front door. When she left, they waved and she returned their goodbyes.

By the time they pulled out of the ranch's long drive, Claire was a blubbering mess.

CHAPTER 26

The next day when Claire woke up, she looked outside her window expecting to see a red-crowned rooster waiting for her. When she remembered they did not have any, at least none that were allowed to wander around the house, she sighed and got back in bed.

She had cried most of the way home, and when they arrived Brad had been waiting in her living room. Without even a hello, she went straight to her room and locked herself in.

Thankfully, that dog she had remembered was real. The moment she walked in the front door, Captain Jack rushed her legs and began barking. The only positive she had seen so far was her faithful dog. The Belgian Sheepdog was all black except for the grey patch over its right eye. Claire had been in a pirate phase when she got the dog, hence the name.

Captain Jack had been her faithful companion for almost eight years. He even got along well with Snickers, her horse.

Claire allowed Captain Jack in her room, but no one else.

Brad tried to follow, but her dad stopped him. "Why don't

you call tomorrow afternoon? Give her some time to come to grips with all this."

"But, what if she won't take my call?" Brad's eyes were on the staircase Claire had just walked up.

"You don't deserve to talk to my daughter. But if she's willing, then I'll let you. However"—Richard pointed his finger closely at Brad's face—"if she doesn't want to speak with you, then you have to respect her wishes." Richard Stapleton was not going to brook any disrespect from Brad. Or at least, not anymore. The lying cheat had proven himself to be worse than a flea on a coon dog, and he would not let the sorry excuse for a man hurt his daughter again.

"Of course, sir. Have a good night." Brad hightailed it out of there as quickly as he could. Without knowing what Claire was thinking, he did not know what his next steps would be.

Claire had been oblivious to what had taken place between her father and her fiancé. Instead, she cried herself to sleep, with her best friend lying next to her.

Lying in bed was never something Claire enjoyed doing. She preferred to be up and about early in the morning so she could spend as much time as possible with her horses. When the thought hit her, she jumped out of bed and went into her en suite bathroom to get ready for the day. The moment she looked at herself in the mirror, she groaned.

Not accustomed to crying herself to sleep, she had not realized how bad she'd look in the morning. She did not just have bags under her eyes, they were full-on sets of luggage. Five-piece sets containing large steamer trunks, and she knew she would not be able to see anyone that day. Except for her animals; the horses never cared what she looked like.

Captain Jack just licked her face and then ran to the door. Claire let her faithful friend out, knowing he would find the doggy door to the back and take care of his business. Then their butler or cook would feed him if she wasn't down in time to take of her dog.

So she showered and put cream on her face and rummaged around in her makeup bag, thinking she must have some sample or other from the department store makeup sales she frequented.

Claire never wore much makeup, but when she did buy it, it was always during a gift or bonus sale. The one thing she did normally do was put on moisturizer twice a day. Those gift sets usually had stuff she rarely used, like under-eye conditioners designed just for covering up bags.

After going through at least twenty different tiny tubes of free trials, she finally found one that was still good. She must have thrown away half of those free tubes since they were so old and crusty. But the one she held in her hand looked to be fresh. She carefully applied the cool cream to the area beneath her eyes and sighed.

While it felt good on her warm skin, it was not the miracle cure she'd hoped for. Sure, some of the giant baggage had shrunk, but it was still obvious. Even if the cream had been the miracle cure it claimed to be, she still had red eyes.

That was one thing she knew she could at least diminish with her tiny bottle of artificial tears. With as much time as she spent riding, dry eyes were an issue at times. When she had done the best she could with makeup and artificial tears, she headed downstairs to breakfast.

Her house was run differently than the Manning ranch. While Judith lovingly prepared every meal for her family, Karen hired a cook. Maisy had lived with them for as long as Claire could remember. Her breakfasts were always great, but she had never once made chocolate chip pancakes. Claire wondered if she could get her cook to make those for her the next morning.

When she reached the breakfast room, a sideboard full of food awaited her. As did the very expensive cappuccino maker she'd made her parents buy a few years back.

Once she had a tall cup of mocha in her hands, she sighed. "Ah, I did miss this." She took a sip before filling her plate with fresh fruit, eggs, bacon, and hash browns.

When she took a seat, her mother looked at her plate and then at her. "Well, I guess you did skip dinner last night. Does this mean you're feeling better?"

Claire looked to her plate and realized why her mother looked so surprised. She did not normally do carbs. Claire had a very nice figure, and though she worked hard every day with the horses, she still worried about carbs sticking to her thighs. "I guess while I was away I developed a taste for hash browns." She shrugged.

"I see. And are you ready to tell us more about what happened? That Manning family seemed very nice, and they have a stellar reputation in this state. But, did they treat you well?" Her dad was not waiting for her to naturally talk about what happened—he was going to get right to the point.

She could not blame him. Since she had cried the whole way home and then ran to her room, they had not had a chance to talk. Claire nodded and took a bite of her bacon. While it was good, it was not quite as good as the smoked bacon Judith made.

"The Mannings are a fantastic family and they treated me better than I could have ever hoped. They made me an honorary member of their family." Claire took a long drink of her mocha and sat back in her chair.

With a piece of watermelon sitting on the end of her fork, she moved it around the small section of fruit on her plate. Then she began to tell them everything that had happened from when she walked in on Brad passionately kissing Gina, to when she jumped on her horse, not caring about the *Just Hitched* sign on the back, and ran away.

Claire did not blame her horse for being scared over the trucker who blew his very loud horn. She understood; her horses had not been trained to ride along the side of the highway, and certainly not trained to deal with an eighteen-wheeler coming too close to Snickers. She mentally reminded herself to grab an apple and a carrot to bring to Snickers when she went out to check on him.

Her mother made her another mocha as she continued to tell her story between bites of scrambled eggs and bacon. Even though she had put some hash browns on her plate, old habits did die hard. Once her mother pointed it out, she only took two bites. Somehow they just didn't taste as good now that she had her memory back.

When she was done, her parents stared at her with mouths agape.

"What?" She wondered if she had food on her mouth or something. It could not have been her story.

"You don't love Brad?" her mother asked.

"Why did you leave a man you obviously do love?" her father asked.

She furrowed her brows. "But, you had to know Brad and I weren't in love. We hardly spent any time together for the past six months."

"Yes, but your business was taking off and we just thought you were doing what you needed to get your horse training to the next level while Brad dealt with the issues of his family ranch." Her mother wiped her mouth with her cloth napkin and set it on the table as though she was done with her breakfast.

"Wait, I thought you understood why I was marrying Brad." Claire shook her head and wondered how her parents did not understand any of it. Then she put her hands up. "Hold up." She turned her gaze on her father. "Did you just say I'm in love with Matthew?"

Her father tilted his head and looked at his only daughter as though she were still a child and totally clueless about everything going on around her. "Yes, it was quite obvious during the few minutes you two were together."

Her mother nodded her agreement. "I saw it in your eyes when you looked at him, and then when you refused to look at him. The pain I saw. At first I wasn't sure, but when you cried the entire way home and ran to your room, I knew. A mother always knows."

"What am I supposed to do? I don't know how he feels about me, and there's such a mess here to clean up. Not to mention my business." Claire put her elbows on the table, then her head fell in her hands.

"Darling, I don't want you to leave the area, but a three-hour drive isn't so bad. And can't you move your business to the Triple J? Surely they'd lease you space on their land to train your horses, wouldn't they?" Her mother stood up and went to put a comforting hand on her shoulder.

"I don't know. Matthew did say something about that before I left. But if he doesn't love me, then what would I do there? I'd much rather stay here if it isn't going to work out with him." Now that Claire had her memory back, she knew she could not marry Brad. That was a given after what happened. But could she and Matthew make something together?

The poor cowboy did not even know who she really was. If he had feelings for her, it was for the person who fell into his arms on the side of the highway, bleeding. Not the confident horsewoman she truly was.

"Sweetheart, shouldn't you ask him?" Her mother's tone

conveyed frustration over the situation, which Claire could understand.

Claire nodded. "I have a few things I must take care of here, and then I'll call Matthew."

That was what she planned, but it was not what happened.

CHAPTER 27

Before Claire was even off their property, Matthew was outside saddling up Thunder. He could not stand around while everyone spoke about his little filly. Correction, *not* his filly. He would have to think about her as some pretty cowgirl who once visited for a week.

Even though Claire had their number, he knew she would not use it. She never did give him her number. If she was serious about keeping in touch, wouldn't she have offered up her number? Or at the very least an email address? No, if she wanted to keep in touch it was all on her now.

The moment he was away from the paddock he kicked Thunder and let him have his head. All Matthew wanted was to get away and not think about the pretty cowgirl who took his heart with her when she left him.

He had to clear his head and get back into the ranch. There was a lot of work to do, fences to fix, cattle to check on, and plans to make for the breeding season. He would also have to check with his sister about when would be best to examine the cattle, to ensure they were healthy and would not pose any problems. Since they had gone organic and did not automatically inject their cows and steers with growth hormones or unnecessary antibiotics, they had had to keep a closer eye on the stock than most ranchers did.

But by doing this, they had healthier animals which in turn meant better-tasting beef.

The horses would also need a once-over to ensure their shoes were in good shape and ready for a rough summer of hard rides. He had plenty to keep him busy this summer, which he was going to need.

When he finally did come in for supper, everyone looked at him with pitying eyes.

Matthew expected Mark to say something stupid, so when John opened his mouth first, he was surprised.

"You know she's gonna be callin' you up soon, and you'll feel like a dolt for mopin' 'round like you are." John chuckled and patted his brother on his shoulder.

"Yeah, buck up, buttercup. It's only a temporary thing. She'll be back." Mark grinned and took his seat at the table.

His family meant well, he was sure of it. But they did not know what Claire would do. How could they? They did not know her very well, and what they did know probably was not the real her. They only knew the amnesiac version of Claire Stapleton.

THE FOLLOWING DAYS WERE A BLUR. If anyone had asked Matthew to detail what he did, he could not. He woke up to the blasted rooster every morning before he was ready. Then he went through the motions each day as he did his job. When it was late enough, he'd hit the hay and fall right to sleep.

He worked harder than he needed to, but he did not mind.

In fact, he welcomed it. Anything to ensure he did *not* think too much about the beautiful blonde woman who haunted his dreams each night.

CHAPTER 28

C laire could not believe how many messages she had waiting for her when she sat down in her office after visiting Snickers. The horse was happy to see her. She knew that much for sure. He even rubbed his nose along her shoulder after she had given him both treats. When she finally walked away from him, he whinnied his dissatisfaction at her leaving, which caused her to smile for only the second time since she had seen Brad and her parents.

Her plan had been to check messages and then take Snickers for a ride before checking on the other horses. But when she saw how many messages she had, she knew she would not get a good ride in that day. She would have to get one of the stable hands to take Snickers out.

She prided herself on riding all horses herself. She rode Snickers daily, but the other horses she rode off and on throughout the week. It was her job to train them, after all. But her hands helped a lot, especially while she was gone.

Her only breaks the first day back in the office were to eat. The rest of the day until supper was spent on the phone or online returning emails. Everyone knew she was getting married and supposed to go on a honeymoon. Word had spread about her disappearing, and a lot of her regular clients were worried.

After one worrisome call, she put on the turquoise and gray sweater she brought with her from the Triple J and wrapped her arms around herself. The comfort it gave her was enough to keep going. While Claire didn't want to need anything, she would allow herself that one piece of memory.

Claire could only imagine what her parents would have gone through if any of her clients had come to see for themselves what was going on. Thankfully, she had informed everyone that her staff were trained well, and they would be able to care for their horses for the week she was supposed to be on her honeymoon.

From what she could tell, no one had made the trip to her stables. She had come home just in time to keep them away. Three of her larger clients did want to come out soon and check on their horses. While she understood, she was not happy with the intrusion. It only meant that she could not leave yet. Not even for a day trip to visit the Manning family...and Matthew.

Her disappearance would have been accepted by everyone if she had told them what really happened. Instead, she did not. She did not want to throw Brad under the bus. But she also did not want everyone knowing her business. Beacon Creek was not the only place that had Diner Divas. If word got out in her town about what really happened, then the old biddies who sat around the hair salon all day gossiping would have found out, and everyone in a one-hundred-mile radius would know her most embarrassing experience.

She did tell everyone that she had fallen off her horse and had amnesia. It was enough to settle everyone down. She even received a few bouquets of flowers with very nice notes from some of her clients.

Which only made her think about all the wedding gifts that had shown up the week before her wedding. She would have to return them all to the gift-givers with notes. She should make Brad do it. Or her cousin.

Then she had to deal with them. Gina had tried calling her the day after Claire got home, but she refused the call. She had also refused two calls and three attempted visits by Brad.

At supper that night, she and her parents had to discuss the situation with Brad.

"I don't know how much you know about the Brown ranch's financial problems, but that's why I agreed to marry him." Saying it out loud made Claire realize how callous and cold the arrangement sounded. "We weren't in love, but we had always been really good friends. I knew that if we merged my business with their ranch, they'd be able to get out from under their debt."

A fork clanked to the plate, and Claire looked up to see shock filling her mother's face. "But...but...why? You didn't have to marry him to help him. In this day and age, there are so many other ways to help a ranch in need. Why marry someone you don't love?"

Claire had thought long and hard about it before accepting his offer. "Because he was my best friend. I had hoped in time we would have fallen in love. Maybe not a passionate love, but a love that would be chosen and built upon a life led together." Now that she thought about it, she knew it was stupid.

"Think about it, Mom. When was the last time you saw me go out on dates, besides with Brad?" It wasn't like there were a plethora of men in the area to choose from. The only good catch was the son of the preacher, and he'd moved away years earlier when he fell in love with a girl visiting family in the area.

Brad was the only single man of quality nearby. The rest were drunkards and louts. She could not trust her business, and her horses, to someone who did not even respect himself.

"Claire, that's just rubbish. If you wanted a husband, we could have helped. We have contacts all over the country. Surely one of them would have been a good match for you?" Her dad furrowed his brow, not understanding his daughter one bit.

"I know." She rubbed her temples. Since she'd been home she'd had a few headaches, but nothing like what she experienced after losing her memory. These were more like stress headaches. "I think it was pure laziness. I want a husband and children, but I don't want to take the time away from my business to look."

She felt shame at what she had just admitted to. Sure, she would have helped Brad with his family ranch by marrying him, but she would have gotten more out of it herself. And in the process kept Brad from finding a woman whom he loved.

Once this thought entered her mind, she deflated with the realization that maybe Brad was not such a bad person after all. He definitely did wrong by cheating on her, but she did wrong by trying to marry him instead of just helping him. Her family had the wealth to get the Brown ranch out of hot water.

She looked at both her parents. "I think it's time I had a talk with Brad." *And Gina*, she thought. If they were truly in love, she was not going to come between them. And she would still help Brad's family. Their two ranches had been neighbors and friends for generations. It was time she acted like a true neighbor and did what was right.

It was not like they had gotten into financial distress

because they gambled the money away, or anything nefarious. Mr. Brown had cancer, and experimental treatments that were not covered under his insurance had cost a lot of money.

Add on a few bad years of drought and low beef prices, and they had just dug deeper and deeper into debt. The kind of debt that would take a generation to get out of. And that's if there weren't any other natural disasters to come along and cause more problems.

She kept going back to the sermon she heard last Sunday. Gossip was not something she ever participated in, but the end of the sermon dealt with forgiveness. She would have to forgive Brad and Gina, then ask them for their forgiveness. She did not set out to hurt them, but wanting to marry Brad just so she could get the family she wanted, and not taking into account that he might want to meet and fall in love with someone one day, was wrong of her.

Two hundred years ago, that type of marriage was common and accepted. But today, love was expected. Her love of all things Jane Austen had probably clouded her thoughts. She would have to cut back on the regency romance novels she read.

Her parents nodded their agreement.

When Claire stood up to go and call Brad, her father stopped her.

"Dear, tell Brad that I'd like to meet with him sometime this week to discuss how we can help them." Her dad nodded and went back to finishing his meal.

That was it. All it took was pointing out how bad the issue had gotten for the Browns and her father was going to help. Had she gone to him in the beginning, none of this would have happened.

But she would not have met Matthew, either.

CHAPTER 29

The next day she met up with Brad after breakfast. Claire wanted to talk to her cousin as well, but the conversation between Brad needed to be between them and no one else.

When she answered the door, the unsure look on Brad's face melted her heart. She probably should have told him a little more over the phone. However, she felt this discussion deserved a face to face.

She smiled and tried to put him at ease. "Let's go for a walk. I know how much you enjoy the orchard on our property." It had been one of his favorite places to spend time. When they were kids they both climbed the trees, but once they started growing too big for the smaller trees to hold them, they had to stop.

Their small orchard that was designed to grow enough for their family, as well as enough to trade with neighbors, held apricots, peaches, and plum-cherry trees.

Once they were far enough away from the house to have some privacy, Brad started. "I'm so sorry, Claire. I never meant to hurt you." He held pleading hands out in front of him.

She nodded. "I know. And I forgive you and Gina." She looked up at Brad. "Are you in love with her?"

His eyes brightened, and he looked off into the distance toward his family ranch and smiled. "Yes, I am. I never thought I would be. Growing up, she was always a pest. But now?" He shrugged. "I can't imagine being without her."

Claire rubbed the back of her neck. "I take it you don't want to marry me now?"

Sadness returned to his eyes. "I'm so sorry, Claire." Brad shook his head. "I never wanted to hurt you. I don't even know how this all happened."

She put her hands up to stop him. "Don't, Brad. We never should have tried to fix things this way." A grimace crossed her face. "I'm sorry as well. I should have gone to my dad and asked him for help. He would have helped you out, no questions asked."

Brad gulped. "You have nothing to be sorry for. We both talked about this and thought it would be a good revenue stream for my ranch to get out of debt and move forward in a way that diversified our holdings. I should have done some-thing like this sooner. But when my father got sick, it was all I could do to keep things going." He raised his hands in the air and dropped them. "I know, it's no excuse. I'm the one with a business degree along with the ag degree. My dual degree should have prepared me for branching out the moment I got home from college."

"Don't blame yourself. I remember when you came home. You did have all sorts of great ideas. You just wanted to take the time to get to know the ranch better, and then your dad got sick. It was just bad timing, not bad management, Brad. You have the knowledge to do this. You only need a little help to get you going." She turned around and looked back at her ranch while running a hand over one of the branches on the peach tree.

"My dad said he wanted to help you out. All you had to do was ask and he would have in a heartbeat. I knew that, but I wanted a family of my own." She turned sad eyes back on Brad. "I wanted a husband and children and felt that I was getting old. You know how limited my choices are here."

Brad chuckled. "What, you don't think Billy-Joe would marry you?"

Claire scoffed. "Oh, he'd marry me, alright. Then spend all our money on booze and racehorses. No thanks."

"Yeah, I see what you mean. And I forgive you, not that I really have anything to forgive. I could have said no when we first discussed this. I think I wanted the easy way out, too." Brad knew an instant influx of cash when they married would go a long way toward getting his ranch back up, and then the constant flow of Claire's horse-training business would move their ranch into the twenty-first century without any extra work on his part.

"I was lazy, too." He shook his head, then looked at Claire. "Will you be able to forgive Gina?"

"Of course." If she could forgive Brad, then she had to forgive Gina, too. It was the right thing to do. The godly thing to do.

CHAPTER 30

A week after Claire left, Matthew worked himself to the bone from sunup to well past sundown. All he did was work, sleep, and eat enough to keep going.

One morning after breakfast, his ma asked him to stay behind and help with the dishes. He never said no to helping her out. They all took turns helping in the kitchen, especially when she asked.

Silently, he began to clear the dishes away from the table and took them to the sink to begin the rinsing. They had a dishwasher they used on a daily basis. But with so many dishes, they tended to wash the pots and pans by hand so they could fill the dishwasher with plates, bowls, glasses, silverware, and the like. By washing the larger items by hand, it left more room in the dishwasher and they did not need to run it after every meal. Usually, just once a day worked for them.

"Son, we need to talk." Judith brought two mugs of fresh coffee to the table and sat down, waiting for her oldest child to join her.

Not knowing what he had done wrong, Matthew thought over the past few days and wondered if he had forgotten something. He did not think he'd forgotten a birthday or his parents' anniversary, did he?

When he rubbed his chin, he realized he had not shaved since *she* left. It had become easier to not name her, and only refer to her when he had to as a personal pronoun. It made her less real and more like a distant memory than anything else.

After he sat down, he thanked his ma for the mug of much-needed coffee. "What did I do wrong?" He was not in the mood to beat around the bush or mince words. He just wanted to get it out in the open and move on. He had a lot of work to do.

Judith chuckled. "Right to the heart of the matter, huh?"

He nodded and chugged his coffee. It scalded his mouth and throat as it went down, but the pain was nothing compared to how he had felt for the past week.

"Alright, then. Your father and I didn't raise a quitter." She stopped to let it sink in and took a drink of her coffee.

Judith watched the pain and then anger as it crossed his face. When his eyes looked down to the table, that's when she knew he was ready for the next part.

"You need to go after her." It was simple: Claire needed to know she was wanted and desired. And nothing said that better than a man finding her and proclaiming his love for her. Although, she doubted her son would have ever thought of it on his own. Most men were too dense to consider something so brave.

Not that her sons were chickens, they really were not. But romantic? That took a different sort of bravery. One she doubted most men possessed.

"She didn't even give me her number. How can I? And why would I when she obviously didn't want me to contact her?" Matthew had considered looking up the number for the

Stapleton ranch, but decided against it when he considered that she had never even tried to give him her number.

How hard could it have been for her to write it down on a piece of paper? Or take his cell phone from him and enter her info? She never even tried. Why should he go out of his way for her when she did not even give him hope?

Judith sighed and shook her head. "You men. You're all alike. After she came to in the clinic and discovered she had amnesia, what did she wonder the most?"

"I don't know, I guess she wondered if she was married?" That was what he wondered the most, that was for sure.

"Wrong. She wondered why no one was looking for her." Judith gave a triumphant smile and waited for her son to catch up with her train of thought.

Matthew's lips puckered and he stared off into the distance. "So you're saying I need to chase her because her family didn't go looking for her after she left them? Isn't that a bit over-dramatic?"

"No, it's how a woman's heart and mind work. She probably doesn't even realize this is what she needs. Trust me, she'll be happy to see you and will want to come home with you. If not right then and there, very soon after." Judith chuckled. "Haven't you ever paid any attention to those romance movies I watch?"

"Uh, I don't know how to answer that without getting in trouble or sounding like a wuss." Matthew figured if he said he did watch them, he'd be less of a man somehow. But if he said he never paid attention, which was how it always went down, then his mom would be upset and possibly hurt that he never paid attention to something she enjoyed so much. It was a lose-lose situation for him.

Judith chuckled and knew exactly what her son meant. "Don't worry, just go get the girl."

CHAPTER 31

The workdays had been long, but enjoyable. Claire loved her work. It was more like getting paid for doing a hobby. Granted, it was some seriously good money, but she loved what she did so much it did not feel like work.

Everything was beginning to fall into place. The Browns were working with her dad on their financial issues, and she had worked things out with Brad and Gina. She did not really feel like hanging out with them, but she did not hold any grudges. After all, you cannot really control who you fall in love with. Not when it is true love.

Thinking about that had her thinking about Matthew when she was not working, which wasn't much this past week. She had really messed up by not calling him yet.

When she sauntered up to Snickers in his stall, she rubbed his head and mane. "So, do you think he'll forgive me for being such an idiot?"

"I guess it all depends on who *he* is," a deep voice that sent chills down Claire's spine called out from behind her.

She whipped around, wide-eyed, hoping her ears were not deceiving her. When her eyes landed on a tall cowboy with a hat in his hand, her heart beat so hard she had to take a few breaths before she could speak. "Matthew? Are you really here?"

"Yes, ma'am. I am."

The cowboy walked toward her as she stood stock still and waited for him.

"How? When?" She had so many questions rolling around in her head, she was not sure which one to ask first.

He chuckled. "Turns out the Stapleton ranch isn't difficult to find at all. Especially when a cowboy stops in at a certain hair salon and asks for directions from a group of ladies." Matthew put his hat back on his head before he reached her and tipped it in her direction.

Claire laughed. "Yes, I'm sure the ol' biddies who hang out at the salon were more than happy to give you directions before spreading it all over town that a good-looking cowboy was looking for me."

His eyebrows rose. "So, you think I'm good lookin'?" His slow, southern drawl sent shivers up her spine and goose-bumps all along her arms.

"You know you are." For the first time since she got her memory back, her smile made it all the way to her eyes, and she felt pure joy with another human. The only thing that had given her any sense of happiness was when she was with her horses, or Captain Jack.

"Did you miss me?" he asked, hopeful that her current mood meant what he thought it did.

"Nah, not at all." She shook her head and wrapped her arms around him for a hug.

Matthew pulled back after a few moments of holding her close. He tapped his hat up so he could look down into her beautiful green eyes that looked like pools of emeralds.

When he took in her scent of lavender, cut grass, and

horse, he knew he was home. He was going to do whatever he could to win her over. He had to. His heart would never forgive him for not doing everything within his power to woo her.

Their heads inched closer, and he felt his heart skip more than a few beats when she closed her eyes in anticipation of his kiss. His nose touched hers, and he had just slanted his head a bit to get to her lips better when a throat behind them cleared and ruined the mood.

His forehead rested against hers, and she groaned. He would have growled if he had been home and someone walked in on their first kiss like this. But as he was in a strange place and had no clue who was behind them, he kept his desire to throttle the interloper in check.

"Sorry, but Mr. Barnett just pulled up." One of Claire's ranch hands sounded worried.

Claire pulled back and stepped around Matthew. "Buck, this is Matthew Manning, from the Triple J Ranch over in Beacon Creek." She motioned between the two men. "Matthew, this is my senior hand, Buck Sterling."

Matthew put out a hand to the older man in front of him, who looked very nervous. "I'll get out of your way if you'll just tell me where to go and wait for ya."

"Buck, can you lead Matthew to the office and maybe get him some coffee?" Claire smiled at her assistant before turning to the drive, where she heard a vehicle pulling up.

"Sure thing, Miss Claire." Buck looked to Matthew. "If you'll follow me. We have one of them fancy cappuccino machines if you like."

Matthew chuckled. "Nah, I'm a plain coffee man. But thanks."

Claire could not believe her luck. Matthew had come looking for her. When she left his ranch just over a week earlier, she forgot to give him her number and only remembered it two days later and could have kicked herself for not giving it to him. When she would have called him, she had so much on her plate she just could not find the time during the day. She kept telling herself she would call him later. It was always later, and later would come and go without her having time.

Now, he was here and she couldn't even find the time to give him a proper hello. She had asked for this. Her entire life she had wanted to build this business up and have more clients than she knew what to do with. Now that she had all these clients and money, she was not sure it was what she truly wanted.

When the truck stopped in the drive and a tall Texan with an even taller hat stepped out wearing snakeskin boots, she smiled. "Mr. Barnett, good to see you."

"Howdy, Ms. Stapleton. How're my girls?" Mr. Barnett had sent two of his mares up to her ranch while she was supposed to be on her honeymoon so she could get to work on them the moment she returned.

"They're doing fine. Follow me and I'll take you to them." To say Claire was frustrated would have been an understatement. The Texan was a week early, and he had interrupted what Claire deemed a very important meeting. However, she could not let him know that, and her mamma didn't raise her to be rude to clients. So she'd deal with him and get the business over with so she could get back to Matthew as soon as possible.

One hour later, she was finally walking Mr. Barnett to her office for coffee when she saw Matthew sitting in front of her cappuccino maker, frowning. Claire chuckled. "What's wrong, Matthew? You look like a kid who's just discovered the tooth fairy isn't real."

"Oh, he's real alright. But this"—he pointed to the offending machine—"makes the strangest coffee I've ever tasted."

She walked over to check that he had not messed with her little baby. She made a cappuccino and tasted it. "Mmmm, tastes just right to me."

Mr. Barnett had stood in the background and watched the two of them interact. "Let me guess, you're a black coffee type o' man?" he asked in a strong southern drawl.

Matthew grinned at the older cowboy and tipped his hat. "Matthew Manning. And yes, black coffee is all a good cowboy ever needs."

"You got that right. But sometimes a good cowgirl likes a froufrou drink." Mr. Barnett stepped farther in and held out his hand. "Steve Barnett, nice to meet ya."

The two cowboys shook hands and smiled at each other, instantly bonding over the need for a good, strong cup of black coffee. No sugar, and certainly no creamer.

"Please, I bet neither of you have ever had a cappuccino or mocha before." Claire raised the cup in her hand and took a sip before smiling at the cowboys in her office. "I'd be happy to make you both one. You know, so you can experience something new?"

"Thanks, but no thanks, ma'am. I'm good with just plain 'ol joe." Mr. Barnett nodded to the machine. "Do ya have plain coffee?"

Claire chuckled and made coffee for each of the cowboys in her office using her K-cup machine.

After another thirty minutes or so of shooting the breeze, Mr. Barnett left saying he could find his own way back to his truck. She should see to the man who had patiently waited in her office for her.

Now that they were alone, her nerves were firing on all

cylinders. Since she had not expected to see him when he showed up earlier, she was excited. But now that she knew he was here for her, and he had almost kissed her earlier, she was as nervous as a new foal and had no idea what to say…or do.

The elephant in the room was about to trample over Matthew, and he felt his chest heaving in an effort to get air. He had come to the Stapleton ranch with a plan, and he needed to clear his head and get on with it.

"Claire, I know you had some things to deal with when you left the Triple J. Have you taken care of them?" Matthew's hopeful heart waited for her response.

She bit her lower lip and sighed. "Yes, and no." The situation with Brad was settled, she knew that much for sure. But the business aspects? She had not had time to consider the real possibility of a move so far. Moving her business to the ranch next door was one thing, but a three-hour drive away, that was very different.

"Claire, are you still engaged?" Before Matthew could do anything else, he had to know the situation with Brad. He would still fight for her until she was married, but how he went about that would have to change if she still planned to marry a man she did not love.

She licked her lips and looked him straight in the eyes. "No. I realized my mistake in trying to force a marriage between two people who were not in love." She chuckled. "I think Brad's going to marry my cousin, but I haven't really spoken to them about it."

Matthew took the three steps needed to stand directly in front of her. "I'm sorry. While I don't understand why you wanted to marry him, I'm sorry if you were hurt in the whole situation." He took her hands in his and squeezed them in comfort.

She did not know why, but she felt her eyes tear up and

her nose itched. If she weren't careful, she would start crying. And she had cried enough over Brad.

Matthew saw the emotion in her eyes and his heart went out to her. If that Brad character were there at that moment, he was not sure he could have stopped himself from punching the guy. A very small part of him wanted to go find the sorry excuse for a man and beat some sense into him. How could anyone *not* love Claire?

But he knew better. While hitting Brad would make him feel better for a few moments, it would not last. Then the guilt would take over and it would spiral down. Besides, he doubted Claire would be happy with him. No matter how much Brad hurt her, she was not the sort of woman who appreciated such displays of testosterone.

Instead, he pulled her to him and held her tightly, letting her cry on his shoulder. Quite literally.

The warmth of Matthew's chest enveloped Claire, and she held tightly to the feeling of *home*. Even though she had known Brad her entire life, she never felt like this when he held her. If she had not been so busy building her business and not even paying attention to anyone else, she would have known something was missing from her relationship with Brad right away.

Brad had been her best friend growing up. Sure, they had kissed a few times as teens, just to see what it was like. But both knew there were not any butterflies when they kissed, and they went back to being best friends after an awkward time passed.

When he came home from college and hugged her, she felt happy, but it was not a feeling of belonging. Nothing at all like when Matthew was near her, let alone when he touched her.

The first time he helped her down from Whiskers came to

her mind, and the feeling she had when his hands wrapped around her waist caused her heart to stutter, and not for the first time. Every time he touched her, her body responded in a way she had never experienced, and probably never would again with anyone else.

Claire pulled back a little, just enough to turn her head up so she could look into Matthew's face. "Why did you come here?" She took in a deep breath and enjoyed his leather and spice scent as it enveloped her senses.

"For this." He looked intently into her eyes and put his large, callused hands on her cheeks and pulled her face toward his.

When their lips met, they both gasped at the electric connection they felt.

Claire's body zinged with excitement and surprise.

When Matthew deepened the kiss, he let out a moan of pure pleasure and thanked God for the woman in arms before he lost all train of thought.

They both wrapped their arms around each other and leaned even more into their kiss. Eventually, Matthew slowed it down. When he pulled back, he took in several large gulps of air, not knowing how he was going to move forward without her if she did not go home with him.

He leaned his forehead down on hers, and a slow smile crossed his lips. "That was better than I had ever thought possible."

Claire's arms had been wrapped around his waist during the most intense kiss she had ever had. She brought her hands to his sides and squeezed. "I wholeheartedly agree."

Her breathless words caused Matthew's chest to burst with pride. He could not believe she was as into the kiss as he had been, and still was. His heart had barely slowed down the sprint it had been doing. If he wasn't careful, he would end up dying from a heart attack. But what a wonderful way to go.

Neither wanted to let go, so they stood there trying to get their breathing under control.

When their eyes met again, Matthew knew without a shadow of a doubt what he was going to do. It was not planned, but surely this type of thing was better coming straight from the heart, wasn't it?

CHAPTER 32

When Matthew bent down on one knee and held her hands in his, she just about cried. Even though it had only been a little over two weeks since they first met, she knew exactly what she wanted. Never in a million years did she think he would want it so quickly. She had hoped he would want it soon, but she was shocked he was down on one knee.

Then her practical side kicked in, and she realized it was not what she had hoped. He probably just wanted to ask something else. Because surely he would not already have a ring and have planned this, would he?

"Claire, I know this is really fast." He chuckled and felt a drop of sweat bead on his forehead and threaten to come down his face. He took one hand out of hers and swiped his forehead after taking his hat off and putting it on the desk next to them.

She gulped, and her chest beat with the anticipation of what he might say next.

"If you want to wait, I understand. But I want you to know how much I love you and want to spend the rest of my life with you. This past week without you has been the worst in my entire life. Even my family knows how I feel about you." Matthew took a breath and smiled at the beautiful woman standing before him.

"The week we had together showed me why my parents have made it work so well this entire time. I want to spend the rest of our lives working together on the ranch and loving each other. Raising our own children to love the land, and the animals." He smiled when he noticed how big Claire's smile was. "And I want to raise a cowgirl who looks just like you and will learn to train horses as well as everything I've heard about you."

Claire could not help herself. She grabbed ahold of his hands and tried to pull him up. She wanted to hold him and say she loved him too, but he stood his ground. Or rather, stayed on his knee, as it were. It did not matter; she would say yes, and he would kiss her again. That was all that mattered. His pretty words were nice, but she doubted she would remember anything other than the fact that he was asking what she'd hoped for, and he was going to kiss her again.

"Claire Stapleton, will you marry me and make me the happiest cowboy in the world?" Matthew waited with bated breath as Claire's mouth moved, but nothing came out.

Yes, yes. A thousand times, yes, was rolling around her head. But nothing would come out. When she tried to talk, a squeak finally made it out. She cleared her throat and tried again. But as before, nothing. So she gave up trying to speak and nodded enthusiastically her consent to be his wife. And for him to be her husband.

"Is that a yes?" Matthew could not hear any words coming from her mouth, but with that smile all over her face and the nodding up and down, he hoped it was the answer he wanted.

"Yes," she finally got out.

He jumped to his feet and wrapped her in his arms and kissed her like there was no tomorrow.

Time flew by and stood still all at once. Claire knew she was in heaven and never wanted to leave again.

An odd sound came from behind her, but she tried to ignore it. As it got louder and louder, her conscious mind told her someone was trying to get them to pull apart.

When she came back down to Earth, she heard the unmistakable sound of her father yelling her name.

"Claire, who is this man and why does he have his mouth on yours?" The stern question from her father caused her to laugh hysterically.

Captain Jack ran into the room barking and jumping on her and Matthew. She pat her dog and Matthew smiled at the pooch who had stopped barking and started licking his hand.

Claire turned around and put her arm around Matthew's waist. He put his arm around her shoulder, and she realized she fit perfectly into his side. It was as though they were built specifically for each other.

Then Captain Jack sat next to her and looked expectantly at Claire's dad.

"Daddy, this is Matthew Manning." She beamed at her father. "My fiancé."

CHAPTER 33

An excited screeching sound came from behind Claire's father.

Karen Stapleton maneuvered around her husband and pulled her daughter into a tight hug. When she let Claire go, she beamed at Matthew. "Good to see you came to your senses."

Richard Stapleton's loud voice filled the room. "Would someone tell me what in tarnation is goin' on here?" Her father was a tall man, but at that moment his presence filled so much of the room, he felt like a giant.

"Daddy, this is Matthew. The man who found me when I fell from Snickers. You know him." She tsked and shook her head.

"Yes, I do. But what is this about him being your fiancé? You hardly know the man." Richard took two steps closer to Matthew and glared at the cowboy.

"Sir, I'm sorry. I know should have asked your permission first." Matthew took his hat off and put it on the desk. "I actually didn't plan on proposing just now." He looked to

Claire, and his eyes softened on her. "I couldn't wait. Not when I knew she was the one for me."

Claire put her hand out, and he took hold of it and brought to his lips. When he kissed the back of her hand, Karen sighed and put a hand to her heart.

"Oh, Richard. Aren't they so cute together?" Karen tilted her head. The joy she saw on her daughter's face told her all she needed to know. This was a love match.

Richard grunted and sat down in one of the overstuffed leather chairs in front of Claire's desk. All he wanted for his daughter was to be happy, but he did not like the idea of a new man so soon. Or one who lived so far away. "Does this mean you'll be moving to Beacon Creek when you get married?"

"Daddy, I won't be far away. Three hours is nothing." She tried to reason with her father, but he stood up abruptly.

"No, three hours is a long time. Living next door, or better yet, here, is what I think is best. Your business is all set up here. Why would you want to move somewhere else?" The father of the bride-to-be ran a ragged hand through his messy hair, causing his hat to fall off.

"Richard!" Karen exclaimed. "She's a grown woman, and you knew she was going to move away someday."

"But I thought she'd move next door, or into the other house on our property. I never in a million years expected her to move away from Red Creek." Not once did he ever consider the possibility his little girl would move somewhere else. His son had married, and they lived in a nice house on their property. He always thought his daughter would do the same.

"Daddy, I'll come visit, and you can come to Beacon Creek and visit us." Claire hugged her dad and whispered, "Please be happy for me. This is what I want."

He sighed. "If he will make you happy, then I'll try to be happy for you, too." Richard let go of his daughter and eyed Matthew. "But if you hurt my little girl, I'll come calling with a cattle prod. And trust me when I say I know how to use it."

Claire laughed, followed by her mother. But Matthew looked like he was going to be sick.

"Mr. Stapleton, I promise, I'll never do anything to hurt your daughter. I love her." Matthew looked imploringly at his soon-to-be father-in-law.

Richard Stapleton only shook his head. "You can't promise that. Even though I hate the idea of my wife hurting from anything I've done, there are times where I inadvertently hurt her. That's part of being human."

"Then I promise to never intentionally hurt Claire." He took Claire's hand in his. "And I will do everything in my power to make her happy."

Claire beamed at her fiancé and brought his rugged hand up to her lips and kissed the back of it. "And I promise to do everything in my power to make you happy."

Richard waved his hands in the air. "Save these vows for the church."

The group laughed, and Karen led them all to the main house for refreshments.

CHAPTER 34

M atthew was invited to stay the night, and they all stayed up late discussing how and when Claire would move to Beacon Creek. There were a lot of details to hash out since a new barn would need to be erected at the Triple J just for Claire's business.

While she had a lot to do to plan for a move, she also had four horses still to work with, and in two weeks she would be getting two new horses.

"I think I should head over to the Triple J tomorrow and check out the land for where I can build a new barn," Claire announced before heading off to bed.

After breakfast, Claire followed Matthew in her own truck to Beacon Creek. Before going to bed the night before, she had cleaned out part of her closet and filled two large plastic bags with clothes she wanted to donate to the homeless effort Elizabeth had spearheaded.

While she didn't get a chance to head into Bozeman with her new friend when she was staying at the ranch, she knew down the road she would be very involved with the program to help the homeless women being used by Big Bart and his gang.

When they pulled down the long dirt road that led to the ranch house, Claire felt a few butterflies rambling around her tummy. She hoped the family would be happy for their news. It was very quick, but she knew it was also the right thing to do.

Matthew had already parked his truck and was outside waiting for Claire to pull up. The moment she put her truck in park, he had her door open and helped her out.

"Are you ready?"

She took in a deep breath and slowly let it out. "I think so." She bit her lower lip. "Do you think they're going to be upset with us?"

Matthew chuckled. "Not at all, darlin'. They're gonna be thrilled." He kissed the top of her head and took her by the hand and led her inside.

When they entered the foyer, they heard a commotion in the living room. Not expecting many people to be inside yet, since it was not lunchtime, Matthew looked to Claire, who looked just as confused as her, and they headed to see what was going on.

Mark saw Matthew and Claire enter the room before anyone else noticed them. His smile could not get any bigger than it was, and he headed over to the new couple. "I see you got the girl?" He nudged his brother's shoulder and chuckled.

"I did. And we have some news to share with everyone." Matthew nudged his brother back, then looked at the room. Most had not paid them any mind yet, and he wondered what was going on.

"Today's a great day for big news." Mark whistled and caught everyone's attention. All at once, the entire room

hushed and looked his way. Then it broke out into shouts of
hello, welcome home, and *it's about time you got here.*

Claire was a little overwhelmed by the welcome, but also
very glad they were all so happy to see her. Matthew
squeezed her hand and pulled her even closer to him.

Luke came up to Matthew and slapped his shoulder.
"Well, big brother, looks like you lost."

Matthew furrowed his brows. "Lost what?" As far as he
knew, he had won the lottery when Claire had agreed to
marry him.

Luke put a hand out for Callie, who walked over with a
smile a mile wide covering her face. "We got engaged last
night."

The room erupted into hoots and hollers again. When they
finally calmed down, Matthew winked at Claire.

"What time did you ask?" Matthew figured he may have
beaten his brother to the punch since he asked in the afternoon, when Luke should have still been working.

Luke looked down at Claire's left hand and did not see a
ring, and smirked. "Does it matter? I asked. You haven't."

Claire laughed and then tried to cover it up with a cough.
She was competitive and hoped they had become engaged
first. Although, all four of them had won as far as she was
concerned.

Knowing that Claire would be fine with this little competition, Matthew pulled Claire into his side and looked out at
his family who were all gathered, including Elizabeth and
Logan. The only one missing was Chloe. He'd have to Face-
Time her later that night when he knew she'd be home.

"I got down on one knee yesterday afternoon," Matthew
countered.

John yelled out, "But did she accept?"

The room broke out into guffaws and laughter. They all

figured if Claire was there, she must have said yes. And Matthew certainly would not have brought it up if she had said no.

Claire put on a straight face and sighed. "Sadly," she began, "I said…" She made them wait a few seconds before responding, "Yes!"

"Hey, where's the ring?" Luke complained.

"Unlike some little brothers"—Matthew punched Luke on the shoulder—"I didn't plan it out for months and worry over what I was going to say. I just jumped in with both feet and asked her."

"But there will be a ring, won't there?" Elizabeth asked.

Matthew puffed out his chest. "Of course there will be. I'll head to Bozeman tomorrow to get one." He would have gone right then and there, but he did not want to leave Claire, and he also did not think it was very romantic asking her to join him to pick out her engagement ring. Since he had done it backwards, he would pick out the ring he thought she would love. And then ask again, in a more appropriate manner, the next time he saw her.

"Kiss her!" Judith yelled out.

Both newly engaged brothers looked at their respective fiancées and grinned.

Matthew leaned down and lightly kissed Claire. When he pulled back, he asked, "How soon before you can move out here?"

"I'd say as soon as you can get my new barn up." She quickly kissed his lips.

"Woot! She's movin' to town next month!" Matthew yelled.

Claire giggled. "I doubt you'll be able to get my barn built that fast."

Caleb Manning walked over to congratulate the new

couple. "Oh, I don't know about that. Somethin' tells me he'll be gang-pressin' all his brothers and friends to help get a new barn up if that's all that's stoppin' you from movin' here."

Claire could not believe her luck. When she saw Brad kissing her cousin, she thought her dreams were over. Now, she had a fiancé who loved her just as much as she loved him, and a huge family who already treated her as one of their own.

She never thought in a million years that getting bucked from a horse could make her so lucky.

"When's the wedding?" Elizabeth asked.

Claire snuggled into Matthew's arms. "How about a Christmas wedding?"

EPILOGUE

10 years later…

"Each year Christmas gets bigger and bigger," Matthew said into the ear of his wife, whom he held in the living room.

They were surrounded for the first time by their entire family and all of the children. Even Chloe was there with her family.

"Well, if everyone would stop having kids then it wouldn't get bigger each year." Claire chuckled.

Chloe waddled to where the couple stood off by themselves watching everyone have fun. "I really do miss the ranch."

"We have room for you and your family to move back." Matthew would always make room for any of his siblings if they wanted to move home.

Mark and John no longer lived inside the main ranch

house. They had built their own homes on the ranch for them and their families. Luke lived in town with Callie and their kids so she could be closer to the station. Especially now that she was being groomed to be the next sheriff.

And since Roman had his own ranch, there was room. Chloe's two boys would have to share a room with the new baby, but there was nothing wrong with that.

"Yes, we'd love to have you back here." Claire smiled at her very pregnant sister-in-law. She still had some news of her own to share, but if they could talk Chloe into moving back, she would hold off on her news.

Claire chuckled. "I seriously doubt we would all fit in here these days." She was thinking about her news and what it might mean for their family. Not that she did not want Chloe to move home, because she did. But they would have to do some more construction if Chloe and her family moved back.

"Matthew, we'd need three rooms. And in all honesty, I do not think my husband would want to live in the main house. We like our privacy." Chloe loved her family, but she had always thought they were too loud and rambunctious for her liking. It was part of the reason she moved away. However, the idea of moving back to the Triple J was exciting.

Her husband wanted to own their own ranch. And if they could manage it, there was a ranch in the area that might work. But it was not livable. They would have to tear down the house and rebuild it completely.

"Sis, I think we can manage with your boys in one room, and you in the other. It wouldn't be for long, just until we can get a new house built on your ranch." Matthew did not care that the house would be full to bursting with his two children,

Chloe's two boys, and the one on the way. They would be just fine. He loved having the children around. Plus, the kids over at John and Mark's houses would have more cousins to play with.

This was exactly what he had dreamed of for most of his adult life.

"Bro, you do realize that I'm having twins, right?" Chloe scoffed.

"Okay, so four boys in one room. It'll be just fine," Mathew countered.

Claire laughed and shook her head. "Dear, what if she has girls?"

"I thought the scans showed it was most clearly boys?" Matthew was a little uncomfortable discussing the pictures of Chloe's unborn children that she wanted to share with the family and what made everyone think they were going to be boys.

"I take it you weren't listening, were you?" Chloe laughed and shook her head at her brother. She knew he was embarrassed by this, even though he already had three children of his own.

"Matthew, she said it could be little fingers in the way. That they could not get a good enough angle of the babies to tell for sure. Just that they *think* it's two boys."

Matthew put his fingers in his ears and said, "Lalalala, I'm not listening."

Claire and Chloe laughed at Matthew's antics. For a rancher who had seen, and helped, as many cattle and horse birthings as he had, he sure was squeamish when it came to human babies.

Claire put a hand on her belly and looked to her husband. "You know, I think I might be carrying twins, too."

Matthew's jaw dropped and his mind cleared before he fell to the ground on his knees. "Twins?" The look of sheer adoration and love filled his face as he looked up into his wife's face. Then he put both of his giant hands on her belly and smiled from ear to ear. "God has surely blessed us."

The End

RECIPES FROM JUDITH MANNING

Judith loves to cook for her family, as evidenced in these books. And her family loves their home cooked meals. While she loves to cook with all fresh ingredients, and mostly from scratch, there are a few little tips and tricks I wanted to share with you.

Cornbread and Chili are staples in a lot of homes, especially during the winter months. A good crock pot and some nice recipes can help anyone make their own meals. I especially love using crock pot recipes on low and put everything together in the morning before work so that it's all ready to go at dinner.

This cornbread recipe is something I think Judith Manning would love! But it actually comes from a reader who sent it to me while I was writing this book. Dee had reached out and offered to send me any recipes I might want or need. Normally, I make corn bread from a box. I know, I know. Judith would have a fit if she knew that. LOL So, I asked Dee for a recipe and she sent it. When I made my own chili and her cornbread, I knew that this was the recipe Judith would love! And I think a lot of you will, too.

DEE'S CORNBREAD RECIPE

Pre-heat oven to 375 while preparing ingredients. You want the oven hot before you put the bread in to cook.

Use a cast-iron skillet for this recipe and it will come out with a wonderful crust on the bottom and sides.

Place the skillet into the oven with ½ cup of butter, shortening, or bacon grease. (I used butter and it came out great) Remember to put in the skillet before you begin mixing the rest of your ingredients, so the butter is melted and the pan hot before you pour in the batter.

Ingredients:
- ½ c butter (for the skillet)
- 1 c cornmeal
- 1 c plain flour
- 2-3 teaspoons sugar (use more if you want it sweeter)
- ½ teaspoon salt
- 2 large eggs
- 1 c buttermilk
- ½ t baking soda

In a small bowl, put in the buttermilk and baking soda. Stir together.

In a medium bowl mix the rest of the ingredients together. Then add the buttermilk mixture. Stir it all up until there are almost no lumps left.

Pull out the hot skillet and add your mixture to the melted butter. Stir it a little bit, but not too much. You want the butter on the bottom to help give you that crunchy layer.

Bake for 25 – 30 minutes. Use a toothpick to determine if the mixture is full cooked or not, but don't overbake.

Serve hot with butter or honey

JUDITH'S THICK AND MEATY CHILI

You'll need at least a 5 Quart crock pot for this recipe

2.5 lbs of ground beef

2 cans of kidney beans

2 cans of black beans

2 cans of diced tomatoes (I like the garlic seasoned ones if you can find them)

1 can corn

1 chili brick (2 if you like it spicier) You can find these in your grocer's freezer section, usually close to the frozen meats. - Defrosted

½ c diced onions

2 teaspoons Himalayan pink sea salt

2 teaspoons pepper

½ c grated cheese (for topping)

Open all of the cans and include the liquids when you put them all into the crockpot. Don't toss any of the liquids.

Brown the ground beef and ½ cup of onions together in a skillet. Drain the grease into one of your used cans for disposal. You can also put in a pink of salt and pepper for flavor.

Mix everything together in the crockpot and cook on low for 7 – 8 hours.

When you serve the chili, you can top it with grated cheese, salsa, sour cream, or anything else you might like.

I prefer to put my cornbread in the bottom of a bowl and pour the chili over the bread and then top with cheese.

This makes for an easy and yummy meal for those cold winter nights. And if there are leftovers, then they heat up nicely for lunches or more dinners. Enjoy!

CHRISTMAS COWBOY ROMANCE

Did you love Matthew and Claire's story? Have you wondered about Chloe and what happened to her? Then don't miss Her Montana Christmas Cowboy! It's already available on pre-order and will deliver to eBooks all over the world come November 1, 2020! Yeee-Haw!

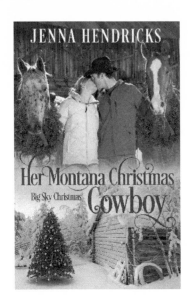

Chloe Manning's first Christmas in Frenchtown was heart-breaking. Will Santa give her her heart's desire during her second?

Brandon Beck left behind a woman for the benefit of his family ranch last Christmas. Now that he's back after a year, why can't he get her out of his heart and mind?

When Santa plays matchmaker, will Chloe and Brandon fall under his Christmas Magic? Or will past hurts keep them apart?

Don't miss out on the first Christmas story of the heart-warming Christmas Cowboy romance series, Big Sky Christmas. Where the romance is clean, and Christmas takes center stage!

First things first, I have to say a HUGE thank you to Dee for such a great cornbread recipe! It was the first time I had ever made cornbread from scratch and it was super easy! I hope you all try it the next time you make chili or anything else that goes well with cornbread! Normally, I just use a box. But not going forward. This easy recipe is now my go-to recipe. Thank you, Dee!!!

This story came to me from God, I'm totally convinced of it. It is my best story to date, and it flowed so easily. This story was supposed to be book 4, not 3. But when I sat down to start writing book 4, Faith of a Cowboy, I couldn't get it going. Runaway Cowgirl Bride kept running through my head. (Puns always intended hehehe) I had already decided on a name and a basic story, but hadn't plotted it out yet. I did have the cover, so that helped me even more.

I changed course and am so happy I went with the Spirit's leading on this one. I'm praying that the same thing happens with the next book!

I think we all have to deal with unknowns in our lives and when Claire lost her memory, it served as a reminder to me that not everything is in my hands. God can work in very mysterious ways. We may not always like how he works, but in the end, the results are what he had in mind for us.

Gossiping is something that's a part of all churches, or any organization with more than a few people in it. But it's something that I've seen hurt people. It's not normally done intentionally, but we can get caught up in the fun of hearing about other people's lives. However, we have to be careful what we say in public, you never know who's listening and what they will do with that information. In the case of Claire, it almost ended up with her being taken by a man who wasn't her husband or even someone she had known. Most gossip won't hurt another like that, but it can hurt people's feelings and it can also hurt their position within a community.

Have you ever played post office? When you were a kid did you get in groups where someone would whisper a little story into one person's ear. Then they would tell the next and so on and so forth? By the time it went through the group, the story always changed. Gossip can do the same. There's a reason the Bible tells us not to have loose lips.

But it's also just as important to forgive. This entire series has elements of forgiveness weaved through it. I have learned a lot about forgiving others, and seeking forgiveness from those I've hurt. It's natural for us to think that when someone wrongs us they don't deserve forgiveness. Maybe they don't. But you deserve to have that burden lifted from your shoulders.

Forgiving isn't necessarily about the other person. By letting go of the hurt and anger, you are helping yourself to heal. That, my friend, is the important part of forgiveness. And the best way to do that is to give it all to God in prayer.

It's only June and I've already started working on the first of 2 Christmas books I'm going to release this year! God willing, they will both release in early November. Book 1 and 2 of the Big Sky Christmas series are already up on pre-order. So if you don't want to miss out on some fun Christmas shenanigans, and you want to see Santa at work in the lives of Frenchtown residents, be sure to pre-order today.

Thank you all so much for reading this far and continuing on this journey with me.

I hope after reading these books with me your hearts are lifted and your burdens are lighter.

God Bless,
   Jenna Hendricks

P.S. I haven't forgotten about Big Bart. I've heard from a few readers who want to know what's going to happen with him. He will be in future books and you will find out more about him, and hopefully see him stopped! I love a good ending. 😊

44023207R00177